Please turn the page for more rave reviews . . .

By Mollie Hardwick

The Doran Fairweather Mysteries
(in chronological order)
MALICE DOMESTIC*
PARSON'S PLEASURE*
UNEASEFUL DEATH*
THE BANDERSNATCH*
PERISH IN JULY*
THE DREAMING DAMOZEL*
COME AWAY, DEATH*

Historical Novels
BLOOD ROYAL
BY THE SWORD DIVIDED
THE CRYSTAL DOVE
THE MERRYMAID
THE SHAKESPEARE GIRL
I REMEMBER LOVE
MONDAY'S CHILD
WILLOWWOOD
LOVERS MEETING
THE DUCHESS OF DUKE STREET
UPSTAIRS, DOWNSTAIRS THREE: THE YEARS OF
    CHANGE
THE WAR TO END WAR (UPSTAIRS, DOWNSTAIRS)
THE WORLD OF UPSTAIRS, DOWNSTAIRS

Published by Fawcett Crest

COME AWAY, DEATH

Mollie Hardwick

FAWCETT CREST • NEW YORK

146855636

Chapter 1

"You are showing signs of wear," Doran said. "You could do with a complete overhaul—possibly cosmetic surgery. I'm totally bored with you."

She ran a trickle of tepid water from the tap over the Chelsea-Derby figurine she was washing in the sink, from its delicate head coroneted with braids and tiny flowers to its sandaled feet, then lowered it to the padded mat beneath. It simpered at her, as did the lamb lying in its porcelain arms, as though grateful for this attention.

"Oh, come now." Her husband, Rodney, had entered the kitchen bearing a coffee cup, half-full of cold liquid because Rodney could never keep his mind on anything but his writing while he worked. "I always rather liked that shepherdess or whatever she is. Not that I imagine shepherdesses ever looked as decorative as that—even Georgian ones."

Doran's ready blush, a girl's blush still, mantled in her cheeks. "Actually I wasn't talking to her—she *is* pretty, isn't she, if only one could hope to look like that after two hundred plus years—except that one wouldn't be here, of course. I was talking to myself, in fact. Thinking how one deteriorates even after forty—well, just nearly forty—years."

It was Rodney's cue to assure her gallantly that she

1

hadn't deteriorated at all, that her slender figure had only been improved by the birth of two children, that her soft curls flattered her small head in their new close cut, and her complexion was still as clear as though it, too, had been laid on not by Nature's sweet and cunning hand, but by a Chelsea-Derby factory painter.

But, though he would once have said all these nice things, which were true, and bestowed a kiss on the nape of her neck, he was conscious that he ought to be getting back to the copy he was writing for a monthly magazine of immense importance to those interested in ancient churches, and he was also aware that he had just quoted Shakespeare, if only mentally. He had taken a vow, at Doran's earnest request, to cure himself of a lifetime's habit of quoting from his massively stocked memory. It was very difficult, but perhaps he could do it if he really tried . . .

Doran lifted the shepherdess out of her bath and replaced her with an ancient Bacchus whose vine-leaves, she noted, were chipped in several places, and some grapes missing. Her antiques shop was long gone, closed by impossibly high rates, and the once charming seaside town where it had been was reduced by property developers to a nasty mess of new offices and flats in already shabby high-rise buildings, interspersed with deserted, boarded-up properties, estate agents, and trashy souvenir shops for such tourists as had nothing better to do than wander about the debased streets, mainly in search of beefburgers.

But many of the objects that had been for sale in the shop called Fairweather Antiques had found their way to Doran's home, Bell House, in the Kentish valley village of Abbotsbourne. And Abbotsbourne itself was changed from an untouched, quiet little place into a rather ordinary mini-town. The omnipresent beefburgers were here too, and charity shops which had replaced commercial ones. The Ross Inn had acquired a great deal of furniture and decoration that nobody could, or did, mistake for genuine antique, while extended licensing hours had attracted numbers of those whose pleasure was to sit outside all day with drinks on hideously uncomfortable benches.

And the church, St. Crispin's, where Rodney had once been vicar: nothing could spoil its beauty, but his successor, the Reverend Edwin Dutton, had had a spirited try. The churchyard was unusually rich in old and historic stones, such as one to a lady-in-waiting of Queen Anne's:

Who served her Sovrain with such zealous joy
As now she doth in Heavenly courts employ.

Edwin Dutton had obliterated this devoted lady's memorial, and a great many others, with a building of architectural brutalism and lavatorial appearance, meant for the use of village children and their minders. So far the children had demonstrated their skill in graffiti-spraying on its potted-meat-pink walls, of such mindless obscenity that even Edwin Dutton had spent ratepayers' money in having the inscriptions removed.

Not long ago the churchyard had housed the victim of a particularly cold-blooded murder, a young drug addict dressed in a parody of Victorian women's clothes. Rodney said grimly that a future unhoused corpse might well be that of a clergyman of middle years and progressive outlook, slain in a fit of retributive rage by a previous incumbent—himself.

Doran stacked the washed china on a tray to dry, made

3

more coffee, and joined Rodney in the living room. He was writing at the dining table as he always seemed to be these days, his silvered brown head bent over the pile of books that crowded round his word processor. It was strange to see him working at anything so technological, but he had learned to use it with surprising speed, and the whispering of its keys disturbed him less than the clatter of his old typewriter.

He was fifty-two, twelve years older than Doran. His thin, clever face was engraved with the lines brought by troubled years: the loss of his young first wife, of his crippled daughter, Helena, in her girlhood, of the long strife with a Church that no longer wanted a scholar-antiquarian putting seditious ideas into the heads of its flock. And the worrying inability of his wife to keep out of situations leading to dangerous investigation ending in murder. Not, so far, her own, but one never knew . . .

He gave her his illuminatingly sweet smile as she entered, pointing to a small figure curled up on the hearthrug, embracing an old, hairy dog blanket. It looked like a sleeping cherub, but was, in fact, their daughter, Armorel.

"Giving no trouble," he said.

"When does she ever? Sometimes I think that child was born with sleeping sickness."

"Well, she was playing with Boris, but he got bored and melted away. Leaving her his blanket for consolation."

"Some consolation! It needs consigning to the flames, but he'd pine away with deprivation. For a foxhound, that creature gives a brilliant impression of a lapdog."

"Crossed with a Saint Bernard. If Kit hadn't saved him as a pup, he'd probably have ended up as dinner for his mates."

"*Chien en casserole.* Doggydins deluxe."

4

Rodney shuddered slightly, his eyes straying wistfully to his screen and what had been a promising dissertation on sculptured wall roods in eleventh-century churches. He hoped Doran had not come in merely to waste his time in idle chat. And she, conscious that she had done just that, guiltily wondered what was the matter with her. She glanced at the calendar on Rodney's desk, which was there to remind him not only what day it was, but what year.

No, that wasn't the answer to the restlessness that surged over her in waves. "You've got a perfect home," she told herself, "a beloved husband and children, enough money as is good for you since that marvelous coup with the Rossetti drawings, good health and presentable looks, even if you *do* go on about them and do things like having your hair cut and layered, which you know Rodney doesn't really care for. You aren't pregnant; Armorel's birth put paid to that."

The arrival of her daughter had certainly been dramatic, even to its appropriate conclusion in the operating theatre. She supposed she had still been under the influence of drugs when she at once insisted on giving her child that fantastic name.

"Armorel," she said dreamily through the fog that seemed to be swirling round her. "Call her that. Perfect."

Rodney, who was finding it hard to believe that his wife and new daughter were both alive, could hardly speak but managed a sort of mew of protest.

"No such name. You dreamed it, darling."

"Yes, there is. Well, there is now."

"School. Think of school. What'll she get for short— Army? Armour?"

Doran smiled. "Robert Burns married a Jean Armour.

5

After her father . . . I don't think it was a shotgun . . . he just didn't care for Burns."

The nurse touched Rodney's shoulder, whispering, "Humor her. She's still under. Say anything."

"If that's what you want," Rodney told Doran, and kissed the baby's incredibly soft cheek. "Welcome, Armorel. Angels guard thee. Please could I have a chair?"

Now, nearly two years on, the name had ceased to astonish.

She stirred her sleeping daughter with a foot, and was rewarded only by a contented small grunt. A new, unpleasing thought crossed her mind. In the two years of Armorel's life her parents had not grown closer to one another: the bed that had been their center had moved, ever so slightly, to a less prominent spot. So to speak.

It seemed to be nobody's fault. One could hardly expect a bridegroom's ardor at Rodney's age. He was in the fragile fifties, after all. The dreaming scholar in him had always needed the space and leisure he was now getting for his academic writings: perhaps it was taking all his energies. Or perhaps what the ballad said was true. "O Love is handsome, and Love is fine, and Love's a jewel while 'tis new, but when 'tis old it groweth cold, and fades away like morning dew."

She hoped not—how much she hoped not. Yet there was a coolness in herself that had not been there before, and that she was deeply ashamed of.

In the garden, beyond the lawn, a patch of crocus blazed in the brilliant sun of early spring, a rich imperial purple, the royal colour of Tyre, stirring her senses to— what? A wild longing for something else, something new, beyond the happy, calm domestic routines that kept Bell House alive, not just a Queen Anne doll's house.

Queen Anne, with all respect, was notoriously dead, as dead as her serving lady in the churchyard.

Suddenly the thought of being dead, past all pleasure, shocked Doran as she had not been shocked for a long time. She turned to her husband.

"Rodney . . ."

"The architecture of late Saxon England," he was tapping absorbedly, *"while rich in individual interest, was haphazard and disorganized in its manifestations. The Norman Conquest brought to it discliplined energy, and a previously unknown method which . . ."*

As Doran spoke he raised his head and stopped his work, with an obvious reluctance that, because he was Rodney, would not vent itself in irritation with her.

At that moment the jangle of the front doorbell interrupted whatever she had been going to ask him.

"Damn," he said.

"Vi will see to it, if she's in." Vi Small, their household help for so long, had been promoted to live-in housekeeper, a post she effortlessly combined with those of nanny and cook. She had even, to increase her usefulness to her own satisfaction, learned to drive.

They heard her voice in the hall, and the deeper tones of a man. Then the door opened and she stood there, as straight and tall and as like a Roman goddess as ever, her hair still a shining black in spite of her sixty years. Vi didn't believe in showing one's age.

"Mr. Evans," she announced, as importantly as she might have said, "The Lord Lieutenant of Kent."

"Howell!" In a flash Doran was in the arms of the visitor. He was shortish, stocky, mustached, his expression one of pleasure mingled with embarrassment. He had been Doran's business partner in Fairweather Antiques,

7

her aide and ally in many adventures, her son's god-father, and trusted friend of all the family.

"Well, now," he said, disengaging himself from her embrace, "*there's* a welcome in the valleys." His voice was as uncompromisingly Welsh as ever, though he had been for years a member of one of London's most famous auction houses. "Hi, Rodney."

"Hi." Rodney detached his gaze from the word processor. This was obviously not his day for early Norman architecture, and he was genuinely pleased to see Howell. "So what are you doing in these rural solitudes, far from the glittering of the gavel and the siren song of the auctioneer?"

"Yes, why aren't you in town, Howell?" Doran was busily settling Howell in his usual chair, pouring him his usual Scotch, and eyeing the window she would need to open as soon as he lit one of his foul-smelling cigarettes. "Or Tokyo or New York or Florence or somewhere?"

"Well, I'm not needed, see, that's why." Howell took a quick swig of the Scotch and shifted uncomfortably. "Got a free day on my hands, so I thought I'd come and see you. Bab all right, is she?" He inspected what he could see of Armorel for the dog blanket.

"Fine. You'll get a better idea of her when she wakens up. And your godson's fine too—nearly ten and very tall for his age. He's got to wear glasses, though—isn't it a pity."

"Thought you liked men in glasses—turn you on, don't they?"

Rodney looked over the top of his elegant, expensive spectacles. "Oh, they do, Howell, they do. I don't think she'd have married me if I hadn't worn them."

"Don't be silly," Doran said. "I *do* think men look tremendously sexy in them, but little boys, no. Oh well, he's in the choir now, and I must say they do rather suit the Tudor ruff."

"Still got the vicar from Hell, have you?" Howell had been in conflict with the Reverend Edwin Dutton on more than one occasion.

"Yes, we have." Rodney stared gloomily into space. "Every time I see him I break the Command to love thy neighbor as thyself."

The longcase clock in the corner chimed a silvery twelve. Doran had fallen in love with it while restoring it from a sorry state of neglect, and Howell had furtively kept it himself instead of selling it for her: he was a clock man to the bone. Then, from remorse and a burst of affection and pity for her in her then state of poverty, he had given it to her.

She glanced at its beaming brass dial. "Howell, you're staying for lunch, aren't you? Oh, you must—I'll go and tell Vi."

"Well, yes, thanks . . ."

But his mind seemed not to be on lunch, unusual for him. Even when it arrived, he ate the excellent local fish as though it were something bread-crumbed from a supermarket fridge, and refused a second beer. Doran, aware of his enthusiasm for the pleasures of the table, knew that his mind was not on these particular pleasures or indeed upon anything to do with them. Was he ill? Dying of something horrible, and come to break the news to them? Her mind raced through a catalogue of nasty diseases, particularly one.

After lunch Howell refused a slug of Rodney's finest malt, and the customary foul cigarette was not produced. A silence fell, perhaps the first that had ever fallen between those three. Doran and Rodney exchanged a

9

look of complicity that exists between long-married people. *Leave him alone. He'll talk when he's ready.*

At last Howell cleared his throat and began. "It's like this, see. I've left Bartleby's."

Doran jumped. "They haven't fired you?"

"Not they. Begged me not to go. Promised me all sorts. I could have had a gold Renaissance clock, German Gothic chamber piece, lovely thing, rare as hen's teeth. But I said I'd made up my mind, and I have. I'm not leaving 'em for anyone else, though they think I am."

"You're starting a gallery of your own?"

Howell snorted. "What? The way things are? Owners going bust and topping theirselves. Not likely. No, I want out of the whole racket. Megamoney, megapeople who don't like me anyway 'cept for what I know, which is more than they do. It's a dirty game now. Well, *you* know that."

"But—"

Howell hurried on. "I've joined a brotherhood, sort of a monastery only it's not called that, just a lot of guys who want to live properly under a bit of discipline."

"You mean you . . ." Rodney floundered. One hardly talked about seeing the light nowadays. "You've found a faith."

Howell grinned. "Go on, ask me if I've been Born Again. No, but one day—it was after I'd done a Jap down over a deal he ought to've had more sense than make—I sat down and took a long, hard look at myself. Didn't like what I saw. What a life. Half of it over anyway, lungs fouled up with filthy fags, too much booze—well, Bartleby's got me off that, I suppose, didn't go with their image. The job—well, it's just shifting things around for top prices, making a bit of profit here and there. . . ."

10

" 'Getting and spending, we lay waste our days,' "
murmured Rodney.

"If you say so. Then there's the other thing." He did
not look at either of them. "The boys. I've been short-
changed by enough to . . ." He decided not to say what he
had been going to say. "I'm through with them, that's all.
May be my age, I dunno about these things, but I do
know it's true. I'm on me own from now on."

Doran couldn't help interrupting with a joyful, "Oh,
Howell, I'm so glad! I never thought they were very nice
to you."

"Luck of the draw. Anyway, I'm takin' a vow of
celibacy; it's in the rules."

"Good," Doran said. "But won't you miss your work?
You've always been such a beaver for it."

"Oh, that's taken care of. Father Abbot's got the old
place choked with good stuff and quite a few clocks—
I'm going to look after 'em for him and do a bit of
buying and selling for fund-raising. Use the old brains,
not to mention cash input."

"You don't think," Rodney said, "they might be interested in you for—how can I put this delicately?—
financial reasons?"

"No," answered Howell shortly.

Rodney knew he must say no more. He had known
other converts—and surely this was one—who had been
all fire and zeal to start with, then faded to apathy. They
talked of other things—the abbey's wild and beautiful
situation in the Preseli Hills, the number of Welshmen in
it, the chance to work with his hands.

"Sure you won't find yourself mucking out the
pigsties?" Doran asked.

"Don't care. I get on with pigs."

11

"And Gwenllian, what does she think?" Doran imagined Howell's fantastic and formidable mother finding a lot of objections to her only son taking up such a life. She had wanted grandchildren passionately, and this put paid to any chance of them.

"Oh, she thinks it's great. They won't stop us seeing each other—I'll be free to get around. Only thing is . . ." Howell visibly prepared himself for yet another important statement. "She got fed up—you know her, always on the go—felt Machynlleth was getting too small for her."

"I can well imagine." Doran could.

"Then her old man died—the boyfriend. Left her all his money and I don't know what in shares and investments. So she thought she'd move up to town, give it a whirl. There was this yuppie couple she met, seems they'd come a crash in the Big Bang, found themselves stuck with a flat they couldn't afford in Dockland. Owned by a rich guy who didn't want to live in it. She said she'd take over their lease, just like that."

"Dockland! Isn't it a bit rough?" Rodney's knowledge of London was as minimal as Sam Weller's had been extensive and peculiar. He possessed a book called *Metropolitan Improvements*, but it had been published in 1839.

Howell's mustache bristled like a tomcat's whiskers. "Wake up, Rodders. All that shippin' stuff went after the war, and most of the buildin's. It was the smartest place to live, all them new flats and high-rises and that—oh, *you* tell him, Doran."

"I will. But go on about Gwenllian."

"Well, when she moved in she liked it—river views, lots of pubs. Then she found it went dead at night—no community spirit, she said. So she wants out. Wants to go off with this new chap she's found, the one who owns the flat. Pays for it. Know anyone who'd want to borrow it? No question of buyin'."

"I really don't think . . ." Rodney began.

"I'd like to," Doran said. "I need a change, too."

The two men stared at her, Rodney in shocked surprise, Howell with something very like admiration.

"What you need, my gel, is some more murders."

Chapter 2

"I think the whole idea is insane."

Rodney was tired of arguing. They had been throwing reasons for and against Howell's offer at each other since his departure an hour or so after lunch. There had been early tea, which neither enjoyed, and a disapproving aura about Vi, as she served it: she could sense trouble, and quite often it had entered the house with Howell Evans, as now. Kit had come home from school, a tall, pale boy with his mother's translucent skin and light brown curls and a faintly academic air, which was his own as much as a reflection of his father's. He had greeted Howell with a formal handshake. Sometimes there was news of interesting antique finds from his godfather, but today he sensed adult preoccupations. He disappeared with homework.

Doran returned to the attack. "I don't see anything insane about it. Vi's here all the time; you and Kit will get looked after just as well as when I'm here. Better, perhaps."

"And what about the Easter holidays?"

"Kit's going down to Simon's in Wiltshire. Armorel will be perfectly happy; she always is. And I'll be home every weekend."

Rodney sighed, exasperated. "Then why couldn't we

14

just have a holiday—us, on our own?" He brightened. "We could go to Rome—or Greece. Or there's a very promising dig up on Hadrian's Wall, and I know a pub you'd like up there, with the ghost of a Roman soldier and an excellent line in game pies. What about it?"

"I don't want ghosts or game pies. I want this flat."

"Why? Why, Doran? If Gwenllian found it dull, so would you. You're not really missing murders, are you? The ones we've been mixed up in have been pretty nasty—and you've usually just missed being the corpse, remember?"

Doran remembered. A vicious blow that had left her with a fractured skull, a locked vault where her bones might have been found years after, two women in two separate cases who would have exterminated her as lightly as though she had been a fly—a maniac in the house next door—there was plenty to remember.

"Of course I don't need any more murders. I just want a change of atmosphere. Howell knows what I'm like."

"And I don't?"

She kissed his forehead, where his hair was receding into something like a tonsure. "Of course you do, darling. So let me have this, won't you? Please. I promise none of you will suffer for it. And I'll be all right, don't worry—you heard Howell say the security system on those flats was as high-tech as it can be."

Rodney had no arguments left. He disliked the idea instinctively—who should know better than he Doran's propensity for finding herself in sinister and dangerous situations? But he also knew the insatiable urge for mysteries and strangenesses that was hers, that must be fed.

He knew also that he would not be altogether sorry

15

to be alone for whole days at a time, with only the discreet Vi to interrupt his work. Their marriage was not in trouble, he knew, but there hung about it the faintest shadow of sameness: the familiar face, so familiar that one almost ceased to notice it, the words anticipated before they were spoken, the tiny irritations, the fretted nerves. And, worst of all, the feeling that if their sex life ended tomorrow, he would be faintly, disgracefully, relieved, set free from a burden of inadequacy.

You're a fusty, disagreeable old man, he told himself. You ought to be following Howell into some celibate order or other. You're not fit to be a husband and a father, with a family most men would die for. All the times I've exalted marriage in my sermons—all those young couples I've given hearty premarital advice to: what did it all mean, if I can descend to these depths? to a state that is horribly like falling out of love . . .

Their argument ended, as they had both known it would, in Doran telephoning Gwenllian to accept the offer of the flat for as long as she wanted it.

She left at the beginning of the next week. There were not so many arrangements to make as she might have thought, for Vi took care of everything. Nothing that Doran did surprised her, after so long. She was calm, efficient, with an answer to every problem.

"You'll have to cook for yourself, you know."

"There's a microwave."

"Sure you can manage it? You'll have to learn the hard way, won't you. I've packed a box of frozen foods, and mind you look at the sell-by date. You can ring here if you get into a snaggle."

"And you'll call me if anything goes wrong? If—anyone's ill . . ."

16

"Make more sense to go for Dr. Kinchen, seeing he's next door."

"Well, he *is* semiretired—he might not want to be called out. . . . Suppose Armorel fell downstairs."

Vi surveyed her employer with a long look of appraisal. It contained affection, understanding, and only the faintest hint of disapproval at this latest mad whim. "She'll bounce," Vi said. "Get on with you now and stop fretting. We're not all made of spun sugar."

Rodney, in his present state of guilt and confusion, had made no objection when Doran said that she would rather drive up alone. "Gwenllian will be there; it won't be like turning up at an empty place. And you'll have all day to get on with your work."

But in her mind, a silly contrary voice was complaining that he hadn't insisted on coming with her.

Parting from the children was worst, because Armorel's rose-mouth was turned down, for once, and her starfish hands clung to Doran's shirt. Kit said nothing reproachful, only wished her a good time and sent love to Gwenllian, but Doran saw that he turned away from her very quickly and went off on his bike without a backward look.

"I'll be back on Saturday," Doran shouted cheerfully from the car window. To herself she said, "You better had, you selfish rat."

The Monday traffic was so congested that it would have been possible for a particularly agile sprite, or a particularly lazy bird, to have traveled all the way to London by a series of flying leaps from one car roof to the next. Doran listened to Brandenburg no. 1 on the car radio, became irritated by Bach's total calm and happy sense of the rightness of things—how would *he* have liked to be grinding through Catford on a wet Monday?—and substituted Berlioz's *Symphonic Fantastique*, because it put

17

pictures into her mind, such as the lovely sinister Young Witch and a procession of little black cats following each other up a mountain to an unholy Sabbath. Now, where did that come from? Ah, a book of Kit's with a lot of magic in it.

Suddenly the interminable New Kent Road wore out at the hideous junction of the Elephant and Castle, and she was in Borough High Street, heading for London Bridge. What a curse it was to have a mind overcrowded with literary and historical allusions—how could one possibly drive through this district without encountering Chaucer and the Pilgrims, Little Dorrit at St. George's Church, Dickens's family at the Marshalsea (now only an old wall), Mr. Pickwick and Wardle hunting for Alfred Jingle and finding Sam Weller? Impossible. She turned resolutely from the red cross sign that beckoned to the George, the only galleried inn left in all London— and found herself looking towards where the newly discovered Shakespearean theatres lay, the Rose and the Globe, and the new Globe so lovingly built by Sam Wanamaker, who had not lived to see his creation finished.

"If you go on like this, my girl," she told herself, "you might as well not bother with London at all: just stay home and read." No, no, no, instinct answered. Not home. Just this great City of Escape. Dickens, whom she had just left behind in the Borough, had rightly said that London was awful, if you thought about it. *But it was London—but it was Life.*

The car had crawled its way onto the bridge and was moving faster. Doran allowed herself one look up and down the great bend of the river—up to Greenwich, down to Westminster—and a wave of excitement flooded

18

her. *"Dull would he be of soul who could pass by a sight so touching in its majesty . . ."* Well, yes, perhaps it had all looked pretty good to Wordsworth at Westminster in the Regency, but it looked a thousand times better now, even on a wet afternoon with the water like mud and a flat grey sky lowering. London was there, at the end of the bridge, beckoning one into its bloodstream, and Doran went.

Thames Street, Byward Street, and oh, God, Tower Hill, and there was the strangely domestic back view of the great fortress, sprawling over the space where so many victims had suffered unimaginable horrors. The voice of one of the brave Jacobite lords, dying for allegiance to Prince Charlie, spoke in Doran's mind, saying calmly to a friend, "Hume, this is terrible," being struck with such a variety of dreadful objects at once—and even the executioner had taken something to keep him from fainting.

It didn't do to dwell on such details. Doran had enough difficulty in keeping to her route, hemmed in by traffic and distracted by alluring street signs. Butler's Wharf, Crane Wharf, New Crane Stairs, Wapping Old Stairs ("Your Molly has never been false, she declares, since the last time we parted on Wapping Old Stairs"), The Prospect of Whitby Inn. Doran was cursed with the faculty of visualizing places as they used to be, not as they were, and a dangerous gift, it was.

But she was an experienced enough driver to keep her eyes on where she was going, and follow her mental map, only occasionally glancing at the road guide on the seat beside her. Excitement dimmed with the realization that she was going into what had been Dockland, scents and sights, London's gateway to foreign parts. And now

19

it was changed, sanitized, unrecognizable to those who saw it, as Doran did, with a double eye.

Her heart sank as she passed row upon row of high-rise flats and offices, industrial estates, buildings that looked as though they didn't know their own purpose. More than anything it reminded her of Rodney's video of *Metropolis*, Fritz Lang's 1927 vision of a nightmare mechanical future. To her annoyance her eyes misted over with tears, of homesickness or disappointment or tiredness, and she lost her direction. She brushed the tears away and resorted to the map, rounded a corner, and saw, with relief, a factorylike structure of brick the exact color of tinned salmon.

Copenhagen Court.

Number 52 Copenhagen Court, Limehouse Peach. That was her new address. She stared at it with loathing.

At least there was nobody to tell her not to park in front of the obvious entrance. In fact, there was nobody in sight at all. As she locked the car she made a mental note to have a car-alarm fitted.

It was an unpleasant surprise to find the door not only locked but crowned with a small television screen. She pressed the buzzer labeled 52. A voice responded.

"Who's that?"

"Me," said Doran unoriginally.

"Oah. Push the door, Me."

In the lofty entrance hall was a lift, which at first sight seemed to offer no means of entry. Then a tiny bright light appeared and flashed on and off. Doran pressed it and was admitted to a small claustrophobic box that appeared to be lined with grey velvet (like, she thought, a rather plushy coffin).

A corridor invisibly lit and a door flush with the wall. And suddenly the grey gloom of the day was gone as a

20

familiar figure materialized before her. Howell's mother, she remembered as small, but with a country sturdiness. This woman barely came up to her shoulder, the bones that had once seemed to be made from thin iron now reduced to wire, though strong wire. Doran had seen antique dolls so constructed, wire skeletons padded out with flesh of wool.

"Gwenllian," she said. "I'm so glad to see you."

A brisk double kiss, one on each cheek, and she was drawn into the room. Gwenllian's perfume, though powerful as ever, was now a very expensive one, filling the air in rivalry with the scent of the huge out-of-season lilies in the corner of the huge room.

"And I to see you, *bach*. Sit down, put your feet up. Would you like tea, or a drink—one of my specials? *You* remember."

Doran did. And though she was not given to drinking at such an hour, it seemed a day for breaking rules.

"One of yours, please."

"Good." The drink, produced swiftly from bottles in a brightly lacquered corner cupboard, was innocuous in appearance, like something colored one would buy for a child. Doran drank and choked. Gwenllian laughed.

"Got a kick, has it?"

"Like a—a sex-crazed stallion. What's in it?"

"Oah, nothing much. A drip of tequila and something to soothe the spirits. I often have one when I feel low."

Doran took another drink, and instantly felt a warmth creep through her veins and a lift of the heart. As she sipped (gulping was not advisable) she sat back and surveyed her complacently smiling friend. Sitting as Gwenllian was, the slight stoop that had bowed her shoulders was not noticeable. She wore a gown of crushed velvet, the color of a very dark grape, down to her tiny feet,

21

high-collared and long-sleeved, with a glitter of decoration down one side, from neck to hip. Beads? Sequins? They seemed to be in shapes, these points of light, and as Gwenllian turned towards the window, they resolved themselves into the heads of owls, tiny-beaked and huge-eyed, done in iridescent thread lit here and there by the glint of *faux perles*.

But the rest of Gwenllian was the same, the woman who years ago had come to Abbotsbourne, an elderly fairy of dubious origin, controlling the troubled Chelmarsh household like some unearthly Welsh Mary Poppins, taking over effortlessly a part in the ill-fated amateur operatic society's production of *The Yeomen of the Guard*, and capturing small Kit's affections, even introducing him to Welsh legends. Doran and Rodney had agreed that she had witch blood: Rodney, though grateful and warmly civil to her, had a very slight reluctance to become involved with her, from an instinct that her magic was not wholly of the Christian kind.

Her dark face was a shade more wrinkled than it had been then, more papery, but still brightly made-up with cosmetics that emphasized the dark brightness of her eyes, twinkling like carved jet.

She had saved Doran's life, and that would never be forgotten, could never be repaid.

"So how do you like the new Isle of Docks? or Dogs, or whateffer," she asked.

"Not a lot, so far. But I expect it will grow on me."

"More than it has on me. Swinging London, I thought." She snorted. "I ought to have got Mal to take a suite at the Savoy for me, and had taxis everywhere. Oh, well—we're off to America next month. Now, I've never been there, only to change cruise ships. I'll like that, and it'll do Mal a power of good. Canary Islands first."

Doran gathered that Mal was the flat owner, the latest of Gwenllian's boyfriends, if that was the word for them. They tended to be very old and extremely rich. She wondered how Gwenllian had acquired such a string of them. Was there some sort of club for the elderly unattached millionaire, and did they leave such prizes as Mrs. Evans to each other, with comments such as "Highly recommended, just the thing for your last years"? "Won't make you feel old like the bimbos do"? Gwenllian certainly exuded a powerful sexual essence that was unconnected with her perfume. How was it done, at seventy-something? Doran wished she knew, and was fairly sure she was never going to find out.

Mal's financial status was up to standard. The apartment was spacious, airy (and air-conditioned), had staggeringly wide views over the river and the whole crowded expanse of south London. It was furnished in execrable taste, as though the owner had telephoned a mammoth department store and ordered the biggest, costliest, and most characterless pieces they had in stock. Doran had never dealt in such furniture, hardly recognized what some of it was supposed to be. Among its shiny vastness Gwenllian looked like an elderly Thumbelina who had never escaped from the giant.

But lying back with her feet up and her drink in her hand or on a curiously nasty glass table at her side, she realized that there was a plus side. The huge sofa she lay on was excessively comfortable, as if stuffed with thistledown or technically processed clouds. It was cream-colored, its scattered cushions seeming designed to fit any part to the human anatomy.

Gwenllian refilled her glass before it needed refilling. "Now tell me what has been happening to you," she said.

23

"Nothing," said Doran. "Absolutely bloody nothing." And suddenly she began to weep, childish noisy sobs shaking her, seeming unstoppable, endless, so that her handkerchief became useless, tears dripping onto the cushion against which she had turned her face.

Gwenllian neither exclaimed nor rushed forward to comfort, only sat and waited for the storm to subside into choking sniffs. Then she produced something roughly the size and texture of a dinner napkin and handed it over.

"There, now, you will feel much, much better. Have one of these," she said, passing over an ornamental tin.

Doran murmured something about taking a captain's biscuit, and another sob escaped her at the thought that Rodney would have instantly understood the allusion.

"It's Rodney, of course," Gwenllian said calmly.

"How—how did you know?"

"How can one know? I guessed. Everything has gone stale, dull—oh, there is a word in Welsh for it. I thought it would be so, that time I stayed with you. Tell me if you like."

Doran told her, immensely grateful that there was no need to dot every *i* and cross every *t*. About how Armorel's birth had not brought them closer together, but had somehow made them into more of an ordinary family—it was difficult to explain how. About how the Rossetti money had given them so much in the way of comfort and security and taken away some of the fun and joy of a good sale, or Rodney's getting a small commission. About how much she missed the shop, and her dealer friends, and seeing Howell every day, and somehow she didn't feel like herself anymore.

"And Rodney doesn't love you as much as he did? Doesn't want to make love very often?"

"How did you know that?" Doran was startled, shaken.

24

"Fifty-one, he would be now. Or two."

"Yes." Doran knew that Gwenllian must remember Rodney's brief, remorseful affair with the beautiful au pair Tiggy, and was terrified that Gwenllian would say that this was the same thing, a man feeling his age, wanting a change of partner, bored with his wife's sameness.

But Gwenllian only smiled. "It is like the sight changing. We see things dim that are near, clear that are far. And you have been near so long. Now you are far away, and he will see you clearly again. That is what I think."

As though putting an end to their discussion, she sat up and rang a silver handbell, which sent out a summons remarkably loud and clear for its size. A door opened at the far end of the room and a figure appeared.

"If you could get us a cup of tea, Poll," Gwenllian said. "You can go after that. Mrs. Chelmarsh and I will be out to dinner."

The girl who nodded without bothering to answer was very plain. By a strong light she might have been seen to have distinct visible features or coloring, but in this half-light of late afternoon Doran thought she resembled a pencil sketch rather than a portrait. Neither tall nor short, her shape obscured by an overall, her face disguised by a pair of unbecoming glasses, she gave an impression of total anonymity. Perhaps she was like one of those secretaries in Rodney's old films who had only to whip off her spectacles and let down a cascade of hair for her employer to cry, "Why, Miss Smith, you're beautiful!" But Doran doubted it.

"That was Polly," said Gwenllian. "She does for me."

"You mean cooks? But you were a terrific cook
25

when—when you stayed with us. You made that Welsh bread that sounds like something else."

"Laver bread. Yes, but I don't now. I don't care so much what I eat now, and this frozen stuff is very good. There's a lot of it in the freezer for you."

Doran stopped herself saying that she already had a stock of such delicacies: it would have seemed ungrateful. Instead she asked what Polly's duties were. .

"Well, she cleans and makes the bed and works the washing machine and all that, you know. I could do it, but why should I? I'm old and she's young and there aren't many jobs round here."

"She's a local girl, is she?"

"Born and bred here, in the days when there were houses, real ones, instead of—these. Got a family somewhere here still, though I've not met them. I don't think we'd have a lot to say to each other."

Doran, watching Polly lay out the tea things, was inclined to agree. The girl's face was pale, snub-nosed; she had light, badly cut hair and very ugly hands. She could, Doran thought, have sat for a portrait of one of Agatha Christie's servants, if only she had the ever-open mouth of the adenoid sufferer, which Christie's Gladyses and Dorises always seemed to be. But her voice, when she spoke, was flat Cockney, a rapid whine almost unintelligible to Doran.

"I'll be off when you've finished, then."

"Yes, you do that," said Gwenllian. The relationship of mistress and maid hardly seemed to be an affectionate one.

Doran wondered why Gwenllian, who was so good at knowing all about people, seemed totally uninterested in Polly. When the girl had left she asked, "What's her other name?"

26

"Haddock," replied Gwenllian.

There seemed to be no appropriate comment. The only one that sprang to Doran's mind was that there had been two distinguished admirals of that name in the eighteenth century, and it seemed unlikely Gwenllian would have cared. But if ever a face fitted a name, here it was.

Apparently a cab was calling for them at half-past seven to take them out to dinner. On Gwenllian's advice, Doran chose a simple brown suit to wear (its expensiveness would be visible only to the trained eye) and no jewellery beyond a pair of plain silver earrings and her wedding ring.

"Better not to catch eyes," Gwenllian warned. "Anyone who shows off gold chains and such at night is a fool."

"Is there a lot of crime round here, then—muggings?"

"Only if people ask for it."

Doran's bedroom was spacious, with a pleasing absence of the pompous furniture in the living room: nothing but a structure that must be meant as a dressing table because it had a mirror, a soft, snaky chaise-longue, a vast chair and an enormous round bed. On this Doran threw herself, with her shoes kicked off. The coverlet, of violet synthetic satin, looked as though it were welded to the bed frame, so closely it fitted, but an experimental pull brought armfuls of it sliding off.

Doran pulled it over herself and within a minute was soundly asleep. When she woke, complete darkness had fallen, yet the room was bathed in soft light from the floor-to-ceiling window.

Doran went to look out, star-dazzled by the lights of the river and the opposite bank. It was like being foot-loose in the skies, a dweller in some constellation, points

27

of light wherever one looked: sometimes a lighted boat gliding past, sometimes a window springing to golden life. The high-rise blocks had become fairy towers. It was a new, startling, exhilarating experience. High above it all, in that never dark London sky, a pale slip of moon glimmered.

" 'And haply the Queen Moon is on her throne, Attended round by all her starry fays . . .' " Impossible not to think of Keats on such a night; Rodney would have gone on at length.

Doran smiled at the thought. She felt like smiling. That deep, dreamless sleep of physical tiredness and emotional release after her burst of crying had left her nearer happiness than she had been for a long time. No worries, no regrets or anxieties—just the ambience of the present time, and a tiny frisson of excitement. Like old days . . .

Gwenllian looked her up and down approvingly. "There's sensible. Pretty but plain. I am dressed as a Welsh widow tonight, as you see."

She was all in black, even to a black cotton scarf over her hair. It made her look less like a Welsh widow than something unearthly from her favorite *Mabinogion* tales. Rodney would be surer than ever that Howell's mother had witch blood in her.

The cab, a respectable vehicle with a respectful driver who seemed known to Gwenllian, took them through narrow ways to a corner in which cowered a small building that looked to Doran as though it had retreated to that corner from the tide of redevelopment that threatened to swallow its frail old bricks.

"The Gun," said Gwenllian. "Very old. Full of stories. You'll like it."

"Are we going to eat here?"

28

"No, can't. They've all gone, you see, the river people, the customs men, the seamen. Only tourists left. But we'll have a drink here because you'll like it."

They were in a tiny pub that breathed atmosphere to Doran. After a few sips of her spritzer, a drink for which there seemed to be very little call, she realized that she was getting high on almost no alcohol, but on London, the exotic one, the reviver.

A leaflet lay on the table, giving the history of the pub. She read it aloud. " '. . . regularly visited by Nelson for his assignations with Lady Hamilton. Upstairs is the very room in which he would meet his Emma . . .' and it goes on to say that they also used to meet in an underground tunnel between here and somewhere called Isle House. Do you suppose they did?"

"Frequently, whenever they got the chance."

"But here? Emma was rather conspicuous, wasn't she—especially when accompanied by a little man with one arm and one eye. And covered in medals."

"I expect they both liked it. Drink up; we have our supper booked somewhere else."

The supper was edible and might have been described as fresh, depending on one's interpretation of the word. The two women talked with hardly a pause. Doran learned more about Howell than she had ever known, including his mother's theory that he was now happy for the first time in his life.

"He had a kind of *hiraeth*—that is homesickness, you know—for the way he is going to live now."

"What? Brown robes and sandals, and holy readings over lunch?"

"I suspect he will use as much as he likes of all that, and do exactly what he thinks fit about the rest."

29

"Like ignore it, and never get found out? Yes, that's Howell, all right."

"Men are funny—they don't always know what they want . . ." Gwenllian's tone suggested that she might have a lot more to say about men, but quite suddenly she changed the subject. More than once during the meal, this happened. Doran wondered if she was to learn more about the shadowy Mal, but nothing of the kind emerged.

As the clock crept on, Doran began to feel she had had quite enough to eat and rather more than enough to drink. Gwenllian's painted eyelids drooped: she blinked and met Doran's eyes with a brilliant smile.

"We must go. I had a lovely meal. Oh, not the food, but it was wonderful to talk to someone."

Doran felt that this said a great deal about Mal, whatever had not been spoken. Gwenllian produced a credit card and laid it on the table. Before she withdrew her hand, Doran covered it with her own in a warm clasp of sudden great affection. Its bones were like the ivory sticks of an old fan, covered thinly with chicken skin.

Before collapsing into her huge, exotic bed as soon as they were in the flat, as she longed to do, Doran made a telephone call. Her own number rang eleven times before it was answered.

How far away had Rodney been from it? His voice was breathless as he answered.

"Abbotsbourne 3581. I mean 407 3581."

"Rodney? It's me."

"Oh. Yes. Of course."

"You sound surprised."

"No, no. I'm sorry, I should have called you, but . . ."

"You lost track of the time, I know. I should have called you earlier, but we've been out to dinner."

"Ah."

30

"Aren't you at least going to ask how I am?"

Doran fumed silently as he said in a rush, "I hope your journey up wasn't too bad."

"It was extremely tedious, but I survived it, thank you, and I actually found Copenhagen Court without too much difficulty, and Gwenllian was very pleased to see me."

As if you cared, she thought bitterly.

"Good. Er—everything's all right here."

"The children?"

"In bed. No trouble. Armorel actually said, 'Where Mummy?' after you'd gone, but we managed to reassure her. Kit's been at Paul's most of the day."

"Give them a kiss for me. And you—how have you been? Making progress with the early Norman architecture?"

"Early . . . Sorry, I . . ."

"Rodney, you haven't been drinking, have you? Not that I should talk, because we had a bottle of wine between us at dinner, but I don't think it's a very good idea on your own."

"No, of course I haven't been drinking, except for one Scotch."

"Well, you sound very odd. I'm tired out, anyway. Talk to you tomorrow—if you'll be in?" Without waiting for a reply to the sarcastic query, she added, "Good night," and hung up, slamming the aerial down viciously as she did so, as if violently extinguishing a candle.

They had never had such a cold, unfriendly conversation. Not one endearment, not one expression of anxiety on his part or admission of missing him on hers. Two strangers a hundred miles apart. More, in some ways. There were tears in Doran's eyes as she hunted for a light

31

switch, but she was too angry to allow them to fall. So he was getting on splendidly without her, he was *glad* she'd gone, was he? The truth at last.

As she climbed into the large, vulgar chocolate-box bed, she thought it was probably designed for a high-class tart. That wasn't a profession she had ever thought of taking up, but given the freedom that now seemed to be hers—the Freedom of London, joke—who knew what might happen?

Rodney put down the telephone. He felt an abject fool. He had made himself ridiculous in Doran's eyes, hurt her, and yet been unable to say sorry. How could you apologize for something you couldn't explain? How would it have sounded?

"Sorry, but I'm in shock, and I didn't call you before because I'm entertaining my mistress—the only mistress I ever had."

Doran was wakened from a heavy, headachy sleep next morning by Gwenllian. She sat up, dazed by the strange opaque light, the unfamiliar room, and the slippery feel of the mock-satin bedclothes.

And by Gwenllian herself, hardly recognizable without her usual heavy makeup, looking, for once, her real age. Her olive skin seemed several shades paler.

"I'm sorry to wake you, but I had to ask you something."

"It's all right, I'm glad to be awake; I was having a horrible dream. What's the matter?"

"Last night—was I wearing my emerald earrings?"

"Goodness, no—I'd have noticed, after what you said about being conspicuous. You had a black scarf

32

sort of twined round your hair, and no earrings at all. Why?"

"Because they're gone. Not in their case. Not anywhere."

Chapter 3

Doran struggled against the tide of ugly dreams that still washed over her waking mind. She longed for a cup of tea, for the reassuring sanity of everyday things, after a miasmic night crowded with angry phantoms.

Her body, in spite of the luxurious bed, felt as though she had spent the last few hours like the Princess in the Andersen fairy tale, being whipped by invisible birch rods as she flew back to her tower.

With an effort she concentrated on Gwenllian, perched forlornly at the foot of the bed.

"What are these earrings? Are they valuable?"

"Very. Mal gave them to me—they were his grandmother's or something, Victorian anyway, real emeralds that hung down as far as here." She gestured. "Shoulder-sweepers, he calls them. He'll be so angry, I can't tell you."

So Gwenllian was afraid of this Mal—that was a new one. Doran pulled her dressing gown round her and prepared to tackle the untimely problem. It appeared that Gwenllian seldom wore the earrings, which were a bit grand for what she called her glitz, the sequins and cabochons that adorned so many of her clothes. They were kept in their original case, a silk-covered one with an elaborate fastening but no lock. This lived in a drawer devoted to lingerie, the cobwebby fragile products of Janet Reger, David Nieper, and Marks and Spencer, which would have caused Gwenllian's nonconformist ancestresses to condemn her as a harlot, even at seventy-something.

The case was there, but the jewels were gone.

"And is anything else missing?" Doran asked.

"Not that I can see."

"But you have lost things before?" She sensed a reluctance to answer.

"Well. A few. There was a little carriage clock, and a cupid candlestick I was rather fond of. Oh, and a little needlework cushion, just a tiny thing I've always had. But no jewelry. Nothing valuable."

Possibly not valuable on the open market, but Doran knew too well how easily such trifles could be got rid of in the trade, that complex network of expert knowledge, instinct, fakery, and downright skulduggery. And all the missing objects were small, easily portable.

A suspect easily sprang to mind.

"Polly. Polly Haddock. Have you ever found her— lifting anything? Showing an interest in your belongings?"

Now there was a definite shiftiness. "Oah, no. Polly's as honest as bread. Just a simple little girl. She'd never . . . no, not Polly."

Doran wondered how honest bread was, when one considered the television commercials' preoccupation with what was left out of and put into it. She felt that, on the whole, it was not a bad comparison.

"Well, it seems very unlikely that anyone could just break into here and steal small items," she said. "The security's pretty high. Do you have anybody else coming here regularly—delivering, or servicing?"

It appeared that Mal, when he bought the place, had seen to it that everything mechanical or electronic worked, as far as could be humanly guaranteed, and that any faults would be dealt with at the highest level. (By men in suits, presumably, with enough ID to get them into the Bank of England's strong room, if it still had one.) And as to deliveries, there were none. Gwenllian did all her own shopping, and nobody bearing parcels or goods ever came through the doors.

It sounded fairly dead, thought Doran, with visions of her own ever-open doors, children running in and out, Vi's brisk toing and froing. Dante could have fitted a place where nobody came and went into his Circle of Hell, very nicely. She felt more and more strongly that Copenhagen Court was never going to be home away from home to her.

But for the moment she had to live in it. "Gwenllian dear, would you awfully mind if I had a shower and got dressed? I can't really think straight like this, and I'm never any good till I've had a cup of tea."

Gwenllian was contrite, apologized repeatedly, and went off to prepare breakfast, which in her distress had not entered her mind. Doran thanked Heaven that whatever her own distress or even degree of hangover, what hotels called a Full English Breakfast had priority before all else. Afterwards she would tackle her hostess's problems and her own.

Poll arrived at her usual time and at Doran's insistence appeared before them in the living room. Gwenllian had not wanted to confront her, Doran sensed, and was amazed: where there had been a fiery little Welsh dragon, there was a hesitant old woman. Most odd.

Poll's demeanor was not that of a guilty thing answering a dreaded summons. She sauntered in, languidly stripping off her rubber gloves, hardly bothering to look from one to the other of them.

"Earrings? Whadda I want wiv your earrings? Got me own, haven't I?" Indeed she had, large plastic objects that from a distance looked like familiar bathroom fittings, but Doran decided that her eyes must be at fault so early in the day. "Not sayin' I took 'em, are yer?"

"No, Polly, of course I'm not. I just wondered if you'd seen them anywhere—lying about, you know."

"No, I ain't. Got too much work to do in this place, all them carpets an' that."

Not true, thought Doran, there wasn't enough work to occupy an able-bodied woman for more than an hour a day. She asked the girl whether the earrings could possibly have been thrown out by mistake, with rubbish, for instance, and got a chilly stare.

"They was green, right, and shiny, like them bits on your dresses?" She spoke to Gwenllian as though accusing her of adorning her clothes with the remains of butchered animals. "I'd 'a seen 'em, wouldn't I. Nuffin' wrong wiv my eyes."

Gwenllian murmured something like a disclaimer of ever having suspected Poll of anything at all. With a shrug the girl left, throwing Doran a glance that expressed pure dislike of her looks, clothes, and style.

It had all been unbelievable, like finding oneself in a scene from *East Enders*. And Gwenllian, queen of her own little kingdom, was in thrall to this creature. She was saying, "There, you see, she knows nothing about them. I'll just have to go on looking."

She wandered off towards her bedroom, leaving Doran speechless. Well, at least the unpleasant episode had served to take her mind off last night and the dreadful conversation with Rodney. Now it came with a rush and in horrid detail. Their parting had been cordial enough, if not what it would once have been. Why should he not have expected to hear her voice when the telephone rang? Did he think he had somehow got rid of her forever when her car vanished up Mays Lane? It seemed as if some unimaginable chemical change had come over him, turning him into a different person.

She stared out at the river-scape, which yesterday had seemed so strange and beautiful. No longer was she a carefree holidaymaker, an explorer; she was somebody trapped in a bad dream. And the only way to break the dream was to cancel her plans. She would pack, go home, and find out the truth, whatever it was.

But there was Gwenllian. How could she be abandoned, especially with her new worry about the missing earrings? It would be unthinkable to desert her on the excuse of an unsatisfactory telephone conversation. Doran shook her head vigorously as if to shake the cobwebs out of it, and went to help in the Great Earring Hunt.

Between them they all but turned the flat inside out, without result. The vacuum-cleaner bag yielded no treasure, only a pile of unsavory dust. Drawer linings were taken out, the airing cupboard emptied, vacant shoes turned upside down.

At last, tired and dirty, Doran straightened up.

"Well, that's it. They aren't here. And does it matter all that much? You needn't tell Mal, need you—not yet, anyway?"

"He's taking us out tonight. He'll expect to see them." Gwenllian's voice was flat: she looked old and defeated.

"Oh, well. Wear something specially nice and hope the conversation doesn't turn on jewelry. Come on, it's lunchtime. Sit down, put your feet up, and I'll get you a drink. And stop worrying."

After lunch, plonked in front of them by Polly as though it were the prisoners' last meal, Doran decided to go for a walk. The weather had settled into that grey brightness that is so often the best the English spring can manage. It was very comfortable for walking, and there was no possibility of getting lost, with so many landmarks.

The towering lighthouse of Canary Wharf dominated lesser towers that, incredibly, held the staffs and contents of the national newspapers that had once been the life of Fleet Street. From those impersonal high-rises went out every day a great flood of words. Politics, comment, criticism, sport, everything talked about by everyone from pub drinkers to the chattering classes of Hampstead, had its voice in those towers, which were not Towers of Babel, but something else, possibly more sinister. Doran sighed. Fleet Street had been cozier, a little enclave of printers' ink and old tradition. You could stroll down Fleet Street and know that Johnson and Bozzy had strolled down it before you, had repaired for tea to the Great Lexicographer's house, just up there on the North Side, had eaten and drunk at the Cheshire Cheese.

Still the little City Griffin, Temple Bar's memorial, defiantly held his place in the torrent of traffic, proudly rampant, telling all comers where his City began. But great Temple Bar, once the divider of the Strand, had been banished to molder out his days in Hertfordshire. Life was as unfair to buildings as it was to people . . .

Doran passed on some of these thoughts to Gwenllian over tea. She felt a little better for her wandering, perhaps because she seemed to have had a conversation with Rodney, who would have noticed the same things and largely agreed with her. Conversations these days were largely in her mind, often with people who were long dead or had never lived at all except in the pages of a book.

Gwenllian smiled. "What a lot you know about the past."

"Yes, I do, don't I. Comes of being an antique dealer. I go round mentally demolishing buildings and putting back what was there before. I wish I could—tear it all down, all the ugly modern brutalist stuff, and bring back curves and arches and columns, and cover the lot with nymphs and cupids and acanthus leaves, and rams' skulls."

Again Gwenllian had that odd look of being about to say something and thinking better of it. Instead she said, "Mal's birthday is today. That is why we are having a celebration meal. Wear one of your pretty frocks."

Some celebration, Doran thought, but laid out on her bed a favorite dress of a very pale blue, with georgette side panels that floated as she walked: a Botticelli dress, perfect for a spring night. So that conspicuous earrings would not bring the missing gems to mind, she chose a pair of crystalline droplets that were expensive but unobtrusive.

So Mal was an Aries, was he. Doran was not usually happy with Aries, who tended to be self-seeking and pushy. But they were usually positive—perhaps that would bring some liveliness to the evening. She dressed and made up discreetly, anxious not to dim Gwenllian's brilliance, and used a very spare amount of her favorite light perfume, which happened to be called Primavera.

After six had struck from a peculiarly horrid streamlined clock that, of course, played the Westminster Chimes, she

40

nervously telephoned home. To her immense relief she heard Vi's voice, not Rodney's.

"Oh, Vi. Only me."

"Hello, Miss Doran—thought you'd be ringing."

"Everything all right—the children?"

"Fine. I took Armorel to the playground today and she went on the swings, loved it, her first time too, and we met ever such a nice little girl and her mummy—you'd have liked them."

"Splendid. And Kit—does he miss me?"

"Well, he's a bit quiet. But he . . ."

"But he what?" (Was there a conspiracy among people not to finish sentences?)

"Nothing special. He's doing his homework now. Shall I get him for you?"

"In a minute. How's Mr. Rodney?" Doran hoped her voice was not trembling.

"Fine. He's out just now."

"Ah. Well, could you get Kit, please?"

Kit sounded his normal self, and was obviously missing her, but Doran detected a faint tinge of excitement in his voice, a hint of a happy secret. But whatever it was, he wasn't going to talk about it. After a few more words with Vi, Doran cut the link with her home, with all she missed and wanted, cursing herself for having embarked on this silly, quixotic adventure.

But there was Gwenllian to think of, and the evening to live through.

At her first sight of Mal, Doran felt a wave of instant dislike, even revulsion, surge through her. He was short and fat, not much taller than Gwenllian, whom he called Gwen. His nearly bald head had tufts of reddish hair over the ears, and a few longer wisps combed sideways over the top of his head, emphasizing its shiny nakedness.

41

His eyes were small and damp-looking, and in his largish pink face there was a lot of room for the small, almost rosebud mouth. His hand, which held Doran's in greeting, was warm and clammy, almost sticky. Not since her first encounter with the late, extremely unlamented Leonard Mumbray had Doran felt such loathing, amounting almost to the sensation of opening a bad egg. She couldn't forbear stealing a look at Gwenllian, who was wearing a social face.

Doran noticed, with relief, that they did not kiss, but with quite another feeling saw that Mal's hand was touching, pinching, fondling Gwenllian's bottom.

"Pleased to meet you," he said to Doran. His voice came from that amorphous district she could only call North Midlands—Derbyshire or Lincolnshire, perhaps. It made her feel markedly southern, something she never felt. Us and them. Ridiculous.

A lot of social small talk went on, birthday greetings included. Mal's expensive overcoat came off because he insisted on their having a drink before leaving for the restaurant. The drinks, dozens of bottles, were ranged on top of the mock-Jacobean cabinet, which held a gigantic television set. Doran had a pale sherry, Gwenllian a small Scotch, Mal a straight vodka in an overlarge glass.

"Cheers, dears," said Mal.

"*Iechyd da,*" said Gwenllian.

Doran muttered something indistinguishable which was more of a prayer than a toast.

Then they were in Mal's car, a Bentley that somehow managed to look vulgar. He had given his chauffeur the evening off—"Makes such a hell of a fuss about parking, silly clot. Nothing to it if you know the district."

They were bound, not for last night's venue, but for a newish restaurant described by Mal as "Continental," which Doran supposed had been opened for the delight of top newspaper employees and their guests. If it belonged to any particular part of the continent of Europe, it would be hard to tell which. The decor was bizarre, with a great many potted plants writhing in corners; the headwaiter addressed Mal as signore all the time; the food was indifferent, some vegetables obviously from the freezer.

When Mal was served with the wrong dish, Doran saw a bad-tempered flash in his eyes, which made her fear for Gwenllian. What could he possibly want from the relationship? If it was sex, as it must partly be, one shuddered: if companionship, what could they possibly have in common?

And yet Gwenllian seemed comfortable enough with him, playfully bringing up in-jokes, laughing at his stories . . . He told them well, one had to admit that. He would be a good after-dinner speaker, especially at all-male gatherings. He knew how to get a laugh, how to entertain. He was lively company: perhaps that was his charm for a lonely woman.

It was soon clear that he found Doran a butt for humor.

"So your old man's a parson, is he?" was not a promising start.

"He was, but he's retired now," she replied, hoping they were not going to discuss Rodney.

"Oh, past it."

"Not at all. He's writing full-time nowadays."

"Clever, eh. And you're an antique dealer, like we see on the telly. 'We sell antiques, we buy rubbish.' Eh?" A knowing laugh.

"Not quite. I had a small shop, but the recession forced me out of business."

"Don't know owt about such things meself. I like to

43

know where my furniture's come from. You can get nasty things from furniture when it's old, can't you?"

Doran decided not to resist temptation. "Oh, you can," she said seriously. "I've seen them—woodworm—in an eighteenth-century table—peering out of the holes, waving their little heads about. They're a sort of transparent white, like maggots, and they breed very fast, practically while you're watching them. It quite put my customer off his dinner, which he happened to be having when he noticed them."

She had produced this untrue piece of information while there was a conversational lull in the room, and raised her voice accordingly. Several heads turned towards her, and somebody said, "Yuk." Mal's face was a mask of disgust, and Gwenllian's a mixture of shock and suppressed laughter.

He's her last hope, thought Doran, but I'll make her see how awful he is. She went on, even more clearly. "The deathwatch beetle, on the other hand, keeps out of sight, and the distinctive clicking noise it makes is a love call, to tell its beloved where it is as its jaws champ through the beams—not a warning of death in the house, of course . . ."

Mal looked repelled, dabbing his mouth with his napkin. And there was something else in his face—fear?

"That'll do," he said abruptly.

"Sorry." Doran smiled sweetly. "But you did ask."

It occurred to her that Mal was probably in his mid or late seventies, and not partial to talk about death. Gwenllian rapidly changed the subject with a question about the Canary Islands, to which they were flying next day, Mal replied, and Doran stayed out of the conversation. At least it had kept away dangerous subjects, such as Rodney.

44

It was she who unthinkingly introduced them. Studying one of the restaurant's unattractive drawings of local buildings, hung on the walls with conspicuous For Sale labels, she said, "I never thought I'd find myself in a lodging so near the Tower. How romantic. Remember *The Yeomen*, Gwenllian?"

"Indeed yes. What a turnup *that* was. A murder, no less."

"And a last-minute cast change, nearly as bad. But you saved the day there, with your splendid contralto. Did you know she has a beautiful voice, Mal? Remember your entry song?" She was glad to see Gwenllian's face was relaxed and smiling again.

"I'll never forget." She sang very softly, almost under her breath, " 'Within its walls of rock the flower of the brave have perished with a constancy unshaken, From the dungeon to the block, from the scaffold to the grave—' "

Mal interrupted sharply, "Crown Jewels, that's what I went there to see, nowt else worth seeing. And by the way, Gwen, where's your emeralds? Why aren't you wearing 'em tonight?"

There was a silence that can only have lasted a fraction of a second, but to Doran seemed minutes. All the color drained from Gwenllian's cheeks, leaving patches of rouge and swaths of eye shadow, ghastly against the dark crimson of her dress with its silver embroideries. Her earrings were silver, too, shaped like snail shells.

She said calmly, "I thought I would wear something else, for a change."

"But you promised."

"Well, I can change my mind, can't I? I was named for the last Welsh Princess of Wales, you know."

"Oh, and royals can go back on a promise, can they. I see. You haven't flogged 'em, have you?"

Doran's fingers were clenched together in her lap, under the sheltering tablecloth. So there had been a promise, worse than she thought. But Gwenllian's eyes were meeting Mal's steadily.

"No. As if I would."

"Well, then."

"I couldn't find them. I'd moved some of my things before Doran came, and they must have got misplaced."

There was fear on one side of the table, anger on the other. Half of the second bottle of wine had gone; now he drank off another glass. Perhaps he was that not unknown thing, a rich man with poor origins.

"I don't like this," he said. "Them earrings was worth a bit. A lot. Apart from the sentimental value."

"I know they were your grandmam's—" Gwenllian began. He pounced.

"Were? Were? Where are they now? What are you keeping back from me?" His voice was rising. At nearby tables heads were beginning to turn. Gwenllian's hand, playing with the embroidery at her neck, was trembling. Suddenly she broke out defiantly. "All right, they're lost. We've looked everywhere and I can't find them— Doran knows. Isn't that true, Doran?"

"Yes. There isn't a place we haven't looked."

"I don't believe you!" Mal shouted. "You've sold 'em, haven't you? Maybe to 'er." He pointed at Doran. "Taffy was a Welshman, Taffy was a thief, isn't that how it goes?"

"You've no right to say that!" Gwenllian flashed.

The headwaiter oiled up to the table. "Everything all right, signore?"

46

"All right? No, it isn't all right. I've been robbed. There's valuable jewelry missing."

The headwaiter was pale with apprehension. A scene, perhaps an assault, the police called: he was terrified for the reputation of his restaurant, for his own skin even, if this furious little fat man turned violent. Behind his back he signaled for help. In the kitchen there was a brawny young Cockney who on occasion had acted as a cool and capable bouncer. Already the other waiters were gathering.

Doran tried reason. "Mal, you're being ridiculous. As if Gwenllian would sell something you gave her—she doesn't have to, she's got everything she needs. Can't you see she's telling the truth? Do calm down and let's leave. Look, you're causing a stir. Please be sensible."

Mal ignored her, shook the headwaiter's nervous hand from his shoulder, scrabbled in an inner pocket and flung something down on his side plate. Doran saw that it was a fifty-pound note. Then, awkwardly, he pushed back his chair and stood up. Somebody was already at his elbow with his coat, scarf, and driving gloves.

"That enough? Right, then. You two can get home best way you can." He struggled into his coat, pushed the waiters aside as they tried to help him, and barged out of the door.

Only the thread of taped music was left to break the silence. The few diners left were finishing their meals, not looking at the table where the disturbance had been. The waiters dispersed, muttering. The head one, with a shrug and a strained smile at Doran and Gwenllian, went to a hooded telephone in a corner, and could be heard talking in rapid Italian.

Gwenllian was shaking uncontrollably, too proud to cry as another woman would have done. Doran ordered a

47

brandy and watched Gwenllian drink it with only a token protest. It seemed to calm the shuddering.

"He can't bear to lose things," Gwenllian said.

It was not difficult to decide on the next move. It seemed very unlikely that Mal would come back for them, and if he did, they would not be waiting for him. He had left the car in a multistory car park several streets away. By now he would barely have reached it. Doran summoned a waiter, proffered the banknote, which more than covered the bill discreetly slipped onto her side plate, and asked the waiter to telephone for a cab. The relief on his young face was almost funny, but she was feeling unamused.

"Come on, we're going," she said. Gwenllian nodded. Doran left a handsome tip conspicuously displayed, asked for their coats, and relaxed for the first time that evening.

"What's Mal short for?" she asked. "Malevolent? Malignant? Malfeasant?"

"Malcolm," Gwenllian said tersely, and added something in Welsh that sounded both malevolent and malignant. Her country had been insulted, and no one did that to her.

The waiters, through the glass in the kitchen door, watched the two women leave, and speculated on the probable cause of the scene.

"Jealousy."

"Of which one? The young one was alone."

"There would be a man somewhere. With her looks, there must be; she is a Botticelli." Guido prided himself on his knowledge of his country's art. "The old man will beat her when they return home. Possibly he will beat them both."

48

The headwaiter was Sicilian. "Where I come from," he said darkly, "this evening would have ended in murder."

The previous evening had ended strangely for Rodney. He had been trying vainly to concentrate his mind on decoration in Romanesque churches. It was a promising subject, with plenty of available illustrations, but for some reason his mind kept wandering off it. Doran had been gone only a few hours, but he seemed to have been alone for long, empty, silent weeks. Outside, soft rain was falling, bringing new scents to the garden. He wondered if it was raining in London.

A pity, in a way, that the children were so little trouble. Kit was watching television with Vi, Armorel sleeping like a cherub in a picture, with her brother's old toy hare clutched to her. No point in disturbing her. But he would have liked to tiptoe in, and survey her proprietorially, like a Victorian papa.

He returned to his work. "*Some of the Norman fonts are strikingly carved,*" he typed, glancing at a photograph of one that certainly was. It appeared to be of a large stone jar decorated in a basketwork pattern. A winged pig with a long, furry tail was stepping out of sight on the aspect presented to the camera, the rear ends of other confused creatures just visible. The pig wore an expression of extreme disdain, perhaps for the prostrate human form on which the jar stood, a person lying on its face with its wrists tied together. Rodney tried to think of an explanation of it, and failed. He sighed. The cat, Tybalt, asleep on the fireside chair, stirred crossly.

To his immense relief the front doorbell rang.

Rodney leaped to his feet. Whoever it was, he welcomed the caller, be it one of the medical students from next door or a late charity collector.

It was neither. Under the strong light from the lamp above the door stood a woman of such beauty that she might have been one of the lovely Roubiliac ladies in his textbook, who had turned from marble to flesh and graciously stepped down from her tomb. Her perfect face rounded to a pointed, dimpled chin, her large eyes beamed as though they had been lamps themselves, her pale hair cascaded on her shoulders, the raindrops that clung to it shining like diamonds.

"Rodney," she said. Her voice was still childish and sweet.

He tried to say, "Tiggy," but the name only came out at the second attempt. For she was Tiggy Denshaw, the beautiful, multiskilled Sloane Doran had met long ago during the case of Uneaseful Death, and who had become one of her few women friends.

Until that fateful amateur production of *The Yeomen of the Guard,* when Rodney had played Jack Point to her Elsie Maynard, and the bittersweet story had drawn them into itself. It had been Rodney's only fall from faithfulness in his marriage to Doran, or that other marriage in the distant past to his long-dead first wife. Doran and Tiggy had somehow got all of them through it with exquisite feminine tact, but he had never forgiven himself, for Doran had been hurt.

And now here she was again, years after, and he was saying inane things about how astonishing, and what a nasty night, and she still drove a BMW, did she. Somehow, in his shock and confusion, he had got her into the parlor and was about to introduce her to the cat.

But before he could make even more a fool of himself, she laughed, her own sweet, high laugh, shook the diamonds out of her hair, and kissed him—the fashionable

50

formal kiss, one to each cheek and one, very light, on the mouth.

"Now," she said, "admit it. You're absolutely, totally gob-smacked to see me, aren't you."

"Stupefied."

"Well, all will be explained. Gwenllian sent me."

"Gwenllian—Evans?" As if they had known dozens of women with that far from common name.

"Of course, who else? Oh, you *do* look funny when you're baffled. May I sit down—all right, Tybalt, I don't want your chair, you great selfish cat. It was like this, you see—"

At that moment the telephone rang, and Doran's voice was saying, "Rodney, it's me."

Chapter 4

The beds i' the East are soft, Antony had said. Not in the East End, they weren't, if this slippery purple marshmallow of a bed was anything to go by. Doran woke from a second night of wild, troubling dreams, the birch rods still lashing the Princess's shoulders, the Princess uneasily aware that there were questions to be answered, but not what the questions were, let alone the answers.

First at the breakfast table in the long kitchen glittering with *batteries de cuisine*, she wondered apprehensively what Gwenllian would be like this morning. And was once again surprised by that lady's calm appearance, dressing in a moth-grey velvet bed gown with a tiny ruff at the throat.

"Bore da," she said pleasantly. "I'm sure you remember what that means."

"Yes, of course. You used to say it every morning at Bell House. Kit learned it at once. Gwenllian, how are you this morning? Did you sleep?"

"Very well. Why not? I hope you did, my dear. One egg or two?"

Breakfast proceeded uneventfully, Gwenllian glancing at the headlines of the newspaper she had brought with her, Doran pondering how to get round to what her friend's plan of action was to be. In the silence she began to develop telephone ears, when every sound seemed to be the first ring of the instrument on its wall bracket. Surely Mal had enough gentlemanly instinct to apologize at the first opportunity. Had he already called? No, she would have heard, since there was a telephone in every room.

But there was nothing. In desperation she flicked on the little transistor radio built into the sophisticated fittings of the oven, and a Mozart symphony stilled her thoughts with its gentle, courtly notes.

Gwenllian, without looking up from her paper, asked, "What makes you so nervous?"

"Do I seem . . . Yes, I suppose I do. Sorry. But I was wondering—I mean, about Mal."

The paper was back in place. "What about him?"

"Well—I wondered what time you'd be going."

"Where?"

"To the airport. It *is* today, isn't it? I don't know how long the flight to the Canaries takes, but . . ."

Gwenllian put the newspaper on the table, having folded it neatly. "I am not going to the Canaries or anywhere else with that person. Did you hear me say last night that I was named for Gwenllian, Princess of the House of Deheubarth?"

Doran said, "Something like that."

"Not descended from her, you understand, because I am not myself of the royal house of Wales, otherwise I would have Owain Glen Dwr on my family tree. Now, Gwenllian led her own army against the Normans at Cydwell in Dyfed, and went down fighting. They still call that battleground Gwenllian's Field. It is a great honor to be named for her."

"And . . ."

"Well, I could not let myself and my country be

53

insulted in public by a person and be seen in that person's company again, now could I?"

"No." Doran wondered how many insults in private there had been. Anyone with such angry, suspicious little eyes could not always have behaved like a Galahad. But obviously the public element made a difference, and the remark about Taffy's morals. Taffy equals David. Dewi Sant, patron saint of Wales.

"Besides, I cursed him," Gwenllian said placidly. "It was a powerful curse. You will find it in that illustrated copy of the *Mabinogion* I gave Kit. One should not associate with anyone under such a curse—it rubs off on you, like coal dust. So that is the end of that."

"Yes. I see. But what will you do?"

"I shall go back to Wales. My cottage is sold—the more fool I was—but until I find another I shall stay at a little hotel not far from Hywel's abbey, or whatever they call it."

"Will you tell him?"

Gwenllian looked devious. "I may, or I may not . . . My dear child, don't look so sad. Mal amused me, you know, he could make me laugh, and he took the trouble to flatter me, which an old woman likes. And at my age it's good to travel with a companion, as long as one can travel, and a companion with a lot of money when you've lived as I have. But that was all. I am not hurt in my heart, only in my pride. Now I must go and pack."

What Doran saw disappearing through the door might have been merely the back of a small old woman, very straight but with a telltale stoop about the shoulders. Or it might have been the rear view of a tiny Welsh dragon, clad in its protective scales of grey because their normal flaming scarlet would have been too much of a giveaway, and the puff of flame from its nostrils a mere thickening

54

in the damp river air. This heraldic image was as clear to Doran's inner sight as the human one that had just left her.

Only Gwenllian, calming down from a huff. Yet the thought flitted through her mind, I shouldn't like to be on the wrong end of that one's curse . . .

A clattering in the hall announced Polly, early for once. Her face was paste-pale in contrast with her black eyeliner, so that she seemed to be wearing a witch's mask. The place was full of witches this morning. But at least she was friendly today.

" 'Ello. Enjoy yerself last night, did yer?"

"Not particularly."

"Been surprised if you 'ad. 'E always takes 'er there, Trat Paulo."

Doran vaguely recalled having seen *La Trattoria San Paolo* written up outside the restaurant. "Mrs. Evans told you where we were going, then."

"Nah, I see it on the calendar." She nodded in the direction of a large beach belle wearing a Mediterranean tan and nothing else. "Naff dump, wouldn't go near it meself." She rubbed her thick upper arms, pulling a face, as though stacking the breakfast pots were a herculean task. "S'pose I got the beds to do after I cleared this lot. You goin' as well as 'er, are yer?"

"Er—no. At least I don't think so. I'm not sure."

She was not, indeed, sure of anything anymore.

Gwenllian was troubled by no such doubts. Late in the morning she announced that she was ready to leave and had brought her little car round to the front. She was wearing a homespun, hand-dyed purple cloak reaching to her ankles, with a scarf of the same material flung round her throat. On anybody else it would have looked eccentric in

55

the extreme, like a castoff from Margaret Rutherford's film wardrobe. Her jewelry was inconspicuous.

"What shall I do if the earrings turn up?" Doran asked.

"Phone Hywel's Father Abbot—he'll get word to me." Doran thought of remarking that a man of God might object to telephoning round Wales about a lady's missing trinkets, then thought better of it. The ways of the Evans family and their kind were not ordinary ways. Instead she asked, "What shall I say to Mal, if he calls?"

"He will not call."

"Oh. And Polly—is she under notice?"

Gwenllian shrugged. "How should I know? Do what you like with her. She can run errands for you, I daresay."

"But—shouldn't Mal be asked? Where will he have gone?"

Another shrug. "To an hotel, I expect—does it matter? Now I must be off."

Helping to load neat, expensive luggage into the car, Doran felt a pang of regret that Gwenllian had not shown the faintest sign of concern about her own immediate plans. So had she been just a character in her friend's story, which was made up from day to day, and always to the storyteller's advantage? She would probably never know. But it seemed just a little sad . . .

Gwenllian started the engine, clicked her seat belt, wound down the window, and gave Doran's cheek a quick, cool kiss.

"Goodbye, *merch*. Take care."

Doran stood alone in the concrete forecourt. *Merch*, daughter, that was what Howell used to call her. But she didn't feel like anyone's daughter, or friend. Or wife.

She trailed desolately back to what, for want of a better word, must be called home.

The apartment, which had always seemed ostentatiously large, now seemed cavernous. It also had an
unpleasantly airtight quality. No sounds penetrated it
from neighboring floors; none of any interest came from
outside when the double-glazed windows were opened
after difficult scufflings with burglar-proof locks. Somewhere out there was traffic: that was all.

Polly served Doran's lunch without comment, her earlier friendliness seeming to have evaporated. Lethargic,
Doran stretched out on the seductively comfortable sofa,
the telephone at her side in case Mal called, as he surely
would. His would be the sort of mentality to which it was
right and proper for a woman to suffer for her misdeeds
before all-forgiving Man chose to speak to her.

Where had they *not* looked for the missing earrings?
Doran began to visualize all the corners where they
might be lurking (not that there were many corners in the
place). Down behind seat cushions, within the dense
thickness of the wall-to-wall carpeting, two tiny green-
glittering chandeliers burrowing their way deeper and
deeper into the pile, like forest animals trying to hide.

She followed them until they burrowed their way into
the ground or somewhere else out of reach, and found her
hand touching something that was neither carpet nor
forest scrub, but a texture unmistakably and endearingly
human—soft, silky human hair, with a very faint scent to
it that she recognized. Her cheek was resting on her husband's shoulder. They were at peace, all the mysteries
and worries over. She heard herself say, "Rodney," and
at the same time heard the mechanical bleeping of the
telephone bell.

It was just beside her on a footstool. Instantly awake,
though with a feeling of loss and regret following

57

her into consciousness, she answered with the number printed below the dial buttons.

Rodney's voice said, "Doran?"

"Yes . . . yes, of course."

"I hardly recognized your voice. Are you all right?"

"Yes, perfectly. I was dreaming—I think. I was expecting someone else, someone for Gwenllian . . . But he doesn't matter. What—"

They were interrupting each other.

"I would have rung before, but we've been out—it was a fine day for once, and I thought we'd drive down to the coast for lunch, and we've only just got back."

"We?"

"Darling, you're not going to believe this, but the most extraordinary thing has happened. Tiggy's here."

There are moments when the earth seems to stop turning: this was one of them.

"*Tiggy?* Tiggy Denshaw?"

"Yes. I thought you wouldn't believe it. Actually, her name isn't Denshaw now . . ."

"She's staying with you? At Bell House?"

"Well, of course. I could hardly send her to a hotel. Anyway, she's stayed here before, remember?"

"I remember." Difficult not to remember the moment when a younger Kit had come to tell his mother that he had seen Daddy kissing Tiggy, the slow, awful realization that Jack Point and his Elsie were lovers in real life. The pain of knowing, and of pretending not to know—as they all three did, afraid of hurting each other, of spoiling something that could never be mended again. The murder that had broken up their amateur production of *The Yeomen* had come as a relief, though an extremely well-disguised one, and Tiggy's tactful departure from their home had been the perfect exit.

And now she was back, lovelier, no doubt, in her maturity, timing her entrance for Doran's rare absence from her home. It must have been planned, to the very day. All Doran's stored-up repression over the years between broke out now, and the bitter jealousy she had hidden under a cloak of polite English denial of unpleasant emotions.

She said carefully, "Where did you go for lunch?"

"Lunch? Oh, same as usual—Martino's, on the balcony."

It had been their special place, their day-out treat, and now he had taken Tiggy there.

"I hope you enjoyed yourselves."

"Yes, very much." She was aware of his talking, saying that it was wonderful for Kit to meet Tiggy again, interesting how a child as young as Armorel could instantly respond to a beautiful face, sad that Tiggy's recently dissolved marriage to a Frenchman should have been childless, gratifying that her beloved grandmother should have left her what amounted to a fortune . . .

Sensing a lack of response at the other end of the line, he ended, "But she can tell you all that this weekend."

"I'm not coming home this weekend."

"Not . . . Darling, what's the matter? What's happened? You don't sound like yourself. Aren't you well? Is it Gwenllian? Doran, please talk to me."

"There's nothing to talk about," said the new, icy Doran. "Tell Vi not to let Armorel have too much orange juice. And tell Kit to ring me sometime. That's all." She hung up on him.

He would call her back, of course. Deliberately she took the handset off its stand and put it under one of the great cumuluslike sofa cushions. Then she went from room to room, unplugging each instrument. There, now he couldn't get at her.

Behind the faint, melancholy sounds of the river and the occasional passing of a car, there came to her other sounds, from the past, clear as though they were in the next room. A sweet soprano, a girl's voice, Tiggy's voice.

> *Though tear and long-drawn sigh*
> *Ill fit a bride, No sadder wife than I*
> *The whole world wide.*
> *Ah me! Ah me!*

No, that wasn't true. She was angry, not sad. All those months of putting up with Rodney's indifference, no more to him than Vi or the cat, making excuses for him, playing her part as passive companion, speaking when spoken to. And now the old Rodney was back—or rather the young one—light-toned and eager, the Rodney who could say, "It's a wonderful day; let's go out and damn the work." Back, but not at her summoning.

> *Ah me! What profit we?*
> *O maids that sigh,*
> *Though gold, though gold should live*
> *If wedded love must die?*

Well, it was dead.

She was in her bedroom, gazing unseeingly out at the grey river. It looked like anything but Spenser's Sweet Thames. It could have been a river of oil, or petrol: no swan could ever have soiled its feathers with such stuff. A small industrial craft was passing, a firm's name painted up on its side, but she couldn't see what the letters said. She was faintly surprised at the reason for this—tears were streaming from her eyes, trickling down her cheeks, silent, uncontrollable. There was a photograph of Kit on the dressing table. She picked it up and held it tightly against her breast, and, still clutching it, subsided onto the bed. Her wet cheek made a black stain on the shiny violet of the coverlet. She was conscious of discomfort, an aching back and an arm turning bloodless, stinging with pins and needles. There was no point in lying about, wilting; no point in anything, come to that. Anesthetized with shock, she stood up, carefully replaced the photograph, noted that the dark afternoon had deepened into twilight, and pressed the button that closed all the curtains with one mechanical swish, and another on the wall that flooded the room with soft, faintly pink light.

On her bed table was a pile of books, her companions on any journey. Some were new, novels from Abbotsbourne Library, some old, everything from *A History of London's River* to tattered volumes that had been hers for most of her life, friendly faces in an alien room.

Without particular intent, her hand went to one of these. It was a stout, blue-bound book, crammed with treasures, for it contained the medicolegal cases of Dr. John Evelyn Thorndyke.

He had never achieved the stature of his great rival, Sherlock Holmes, possibly because of his lack of spectacular bad habits. But Doran thought his methods of detection a shade superior to Holmes's, and was drawn to his handsome appearance—he was just the prematurely grey, mature father figure she admired, even found alluring—and his cases, mostly forensic, were deliciously grisly. His author, Dr. R. Austin Freeman, was forgotten now. But not by Doran.

She went back to the living room and resettled herself on the opulent sofa, beside the hidden, silent telephone. Then she got up again and added a bottle of Glenmorangie, a siphon of soda, and a tumbler to the occasional table. She was quite unaware of doing these things deliberately.

Thus, in the company of the benevolent doctor-lawyer, she drifted into an Edwardian world of bachelor chambers, dismembered corpses, bones bought as a student's set and passed off as fire victims, missing gentlemen who turned up as neat piles of ash in metallurgists' furnaces—thus Doran prepared to spend the worst evening of her life. The level of the Glenmorangie sank lower and lower.

There Poll found her in the morning, sleeping heavily, the stains of dried tears on her cheeks, a book lying open on the floor beside her.

Chapter 5

A strong hand on Doran's shoulder shook her awake, none too gently.

Stiff and aching, she struggled to sit up. The shaking was still going on. "All right, all right," she managed to say.

"Time, too. Didn't 'alf give me a shock. Thought you was dead."

"No, I'm perfectly all right." Which was not true. A butcher's cleaver seemed to be bisecting her head very painfully, a taste far worse (surely) than the bottom of a parrot's cage filled her mouth, and a deep sense of shame possessed her. Somehow it must be explained to Polly, who would otherwise conclude that she had simply passed out drunk.

"I had a bit of a shock myself last night," she said. "I lay down and had a drink and then . . . I don't know what happened. I can't remember any more."

Polly's gaze was fixed on the whisky bottle, not quite half empty. It was quite clear to her what had happened, though she was faintly surprised that this airy-fairy, dreamy-looking woman with a parson husband should be a lush. She said, "D'you want some coffee?"

Doran shuddered. She would never forget the effect of

it after one memorable party. "Thanks, but no. Just some water."

"I got somefink else," Polly volunteered. "Proper hangover cure. Like to try it?"

"Please. Anything at all!"

Polly returned with a glass of something that tasted as innocuous as it looked. Doran drank it off, and asked what it was.

"Tonic, like in gin, wiv lemon juice an' a drop of angostura." Doran regarded her with surprise and admiration, this cloddish creature hardly able to answer civilly at first and now producing a remedy worthy of Gwenllian herself. For it was working; the black fogs were rising and the pain of the cleaver-blows lessening.

As she showered and dressed, moving very carefully, Doran thought back to the previous evening. She was used to whisky as a nightcap; she had not drunk herself silly. From what traces of memory remained, it seemed to her that she had blacked out and fallen into what was more like a coma than a drink-induced sleep. It hadn't happened before, and, she resolved grimly, it shouldn't happen again. She had had her dramatic scene: now it remained to live with things as they were, unthinkable though they might be.

One's brain, or at any rate Doran's brain, had an Off button which could be used to make life bearable at black times. Polly should hear no more excuses or explanations.

And Polly should justify her existence. Guided by the whine of the Hoover, Doran found her in a bedroom, pushing the thing up and down the carpet with an expression of terminal boredom.

"Polly," she said, "would you like to come for a walk

64

with me? I need some fresh air and I'm sure this place is clean enough."

"You what?"

"Come for a walk. Show me the sights. I don't know this part of the world. I'm sure Mr.—your employer— I'm sure he wouldn't mind."

" 'Is name's Mal Grover, and I don't care if 'e minds or not. 'E's an old pig, 'e is. Right, I'll get me coat. Oh, and all the phones was off when I come in—I put 'em on again."

"Good. I didn't want to be disturbed last night." Lies, lies.

They made an odd pair as they walked, Doran tall and willowy, with an air that was not touristy, and might have belonged to any of the incomers to Dockland's expensive flats, and Polly, an obvious native, dumpy and thickset, with a London pallor. She was not used to going for walks, still less used to acting as tour guide. She knew only the most basic facts about the area. That was the ter-minus of the Docklands Light Railway, that was Canary Wharf, you could see it for miles and there were guards on it, the IRA had had a go at it, that was Greenwich over there and there was some sort of tunnel under the river that a guy with a French name had built hundreds of years ago, only Polly wouldn't fancy going down it.

Doran recognized Brunel and his achievement, and suggested trying the Greenwich Ferry and exploring the other bank, but Polly shivered affectedly in the light breeze off the water and said it was no day for the river. They had turned up Ferry Road and were heading vaguely in the direction of Milwall. The scenery was less than fascinating, Polly had been right about the cold, and the misery of the previous night was creeping over Doran again. She was about to suggest that they go for a drink, on the hair-of-the-dog principle, when Polly suddenly turned left up a narrow alley leading back towards the river.

"Where are we going?"

"See my uncle," Polly called over her shoulder.

Mystified, Doran followed. Whatever her uncle might be like, and she feared the worst, his company would make a change from Polly's.

They were back at the river, an ugly, nondescript block of offices between them and it, and a narrow cobbled alleyway, its street sign, Staple Lane, just readable. It was surprising to see cobbles instead of the ubiquitous pink brick paving, even more surprising to see, a few doors from the office block, a building that seemed to be an old pub, or perhaps something once even grander.

It was set back from the lane behind a crumbling wall. Small, square Georgian windows, a modern, shabby door with a lintel above it, obviously of another century, and two stories over that in which Georgian gave way to Victorian, but still the ancient bricks, the color of dark red roses that had died and were turning black.

Doran's spirits lifted. At least here was something from her own scene, familiar and picturesque. She followed Polly through the shabby door, up a steep, narrow flight of uncarpeted stairs, unlit and creaky. They stopped outside a door of the farmhouse type. Polly lifted the wooden latch and went in.

The room was long and wide, with a fireplace at one end where burned a small fire in a duck's-nest grate. The walls had been roughly painted—or was it not paint, but old-fashioned whitewash? Underneath in patches could be seen old, dark timber.

The window, set in the middle of the wall facing the door, was small and square, with twelve panes, uncurtained. The only other light in the room came from a ship's lantern hung from the ceiling: an oil lamp, Doran guessed. There was a table under the window, one or two chairs and stools, and a rough chest with wooden knobs. The place seemed to be an unlikely combination of the hold of HMS *Victory*, Mr. Dorrit's parlor in the Marshalsea Prison, and the sort of interior seen in eighteenth-century pictures of cottage life.

The pervading smell, Doran didn't feel capable of analyzing, but fish was in it somewhere, and strong spirits, and dust, and a miasma that was not of the twentieth century. This is what they never tell you about the Past, Doran thought. I have walked into the Past.

In an upright chair by the fire sat a man, only dimly visible at first. Then, as her eyes got used to the poor light, Doran saw that he was big, thinly built, and old, to judge by the quantity of white hair that brushed the shabby shoulders of his coat. At her entrance he made no attempt to rise, but merely turned his head in her direction. She wondered if he was blind.

Polly said briskly, " 'Ere's Mrs. Chelmarsh, Uncle, stayin' with old Gwen. I brought 'er out for a walk, thought it might make a change for you to see 'er."

"That was kind, Poll." His voice was deep, not as Cockney-accented as Polly's and far more educated, but unmistakably of London. It was not cracked with age, as Doran had expected, but mature, almost mellow, with something of the actor in it. "Get the lady a chair, will you."

Polly pulled up a small straight chair to the opposite side of the fire, and Doran sat down, increasingly feeling as if she were in a dream. She murmured a greeting. Polly, saying she would get them a bit of something,

67

vanished through a door in the window wall, like a character in a play.

"I hope we're not disturbing you," Doran said, feeling that light chatter was expected of her. "Polly didn't tell me she was bringing me to visit anybody."

"It does me good to have a visitor. I don't get about much. As you see." He drew aside the rug that covered his knees. The chair he sat in was a wheelchair, the kind propelled along by the user turning the wheels manually. It was a surprising sight in an age of sophisticated mechanical aids for the disabled, and Doran's mind flew to the elaborate, costly electric wheelchair that her crippled stepdaughter, Helena, had used, and the almost equally expensive folding version in which she had been taken to school. Was this a family that had somehow escaped the Welfare State? Where did Housing Benefit and Social Services fit into the household?

Polly was returning with a tray. The contents of the tray were innocuous—two bottles of Bass, a can of Coca-Cola, and a tin of assorted biscuits.

"You can 'ave Coke if you'd rather," Polly said, no doubt mindful of Doran's state that morning.

"Oh no! Bass will be perfect, thank you."

"Not ready for yer usual, Uncle?"

"No, ta, love—bit early for that." Doran hoped his usual was not whisky, and would not be forthcoming if it was. With social brightness she said, "What a very fascinating house, Mr. Haddock. How far does it go back?"

Polly gave a short scream of laughter. " 'Is name ain't 'Addock—it's Slater. My mum was 'is sister, an' she married an 'Addock, see?"

"Oh, I'm sorry. I naturally thought . . ."

"Don't apologize," Slater said kindly. "Call me Bill; they all do."

" 'Er name's Dora," Polly volunteered.

"No, it isn't, Polly," its owner said hastily. "It's Doran—I think I made it up myself when I was a child because they'd christened me Dora Ann, which I thought was pretty dreadful."

Slater smiled. studying her. Seeing him clearer now, as the fire flickered up. Doran realized that he was not an old man at all, though he might be in his fifties. His face was aquiline, with a fine nose and cheekbones, yet not aristocratic in effect. It was as though a medieval sculptor had started out to carve the face of the lord of the manor, and abandoned it to an apprentice for finishing. Such faces Victorian painters gave to fishermen, sailors, Saxon defenders of forts against the Norman foe, that sort of thing. A face for stone, not marble.

Whatever it lacked in perfection was made up for by the eyes. They were so dark that in proper lighting they could have seemed truly black, not brown, and their gaze was fixed on a far horizon. How could she ever have thought him blind?

She could now see that the white hair shaded in parts from snow to pitch. In youth this man had been as black of hair as he was of eye.

In the same moment as she saw all this, something very old and primitive in her raised its head and looked about, seeking its own. On first sight of Bill Slater's shock of white hair, another face had materialized behind his: the face of a past and gone love of Doran's, long before Rodney, someone she had loved and lost—worse, never had. The charming, scholarly Henry Gore, encountered in Oxford when she was serving in an antiques shop. Foiled then, she had met him many years later— yes! And *that* had been during a breach with Rodney.

But that violent attraction had gone unconsummated,

69

and never would be, now, for she had read of Henry's death. And now a man's white hair had raised Henry's ghost, and like Cynara's lover, she was sick of an old passion.

How totally damnable and ridiculous life was.

He said, "You asked me how old this place was. Well, I can't tell you, because nobody knows—unless you do or some of your antiques friends. But it's seen a good few reigns."

What a curious way of putting it, unless one were an ardent monarchist. She looked round the room, trying to see it with an appraiser's eye, which as a rule came naturally to her. The ceiling was low and uneven, timber planks, Doran guessed, which had never been reinforced. High up on the walls, hiding away in the shadows thrown by the lantern were—yes, carvings, blunted by time and obscured by dirt. She said, "May I?" and got up to look at them more closely.

There were mermaids and mermen and what looked like monsters or giant fish, gaping wide to swallow the ships and sailors that tossed on plaster waves. A mermaid was laughing as she dragged down a ship by its rope. And other forms, men in flight or perhaps a running crowd, and somebody seated high on a throne? Perhaps a king, more likely a divine personage. In another place, other dry-land monsters, a recognizable dragon and a very fierce-looking boar, with a lot of teeth and bristles and a formidable snout.

"What do these figures mean?" Doran asked.

"Your guess is as good as mine. Only I remember they was once colored."

At another time Doran would have been tempted to air her considerable knowledge of heraldry, but something kept her quiet. One didn't lecture in a museum. She had been kneeling on a stool to see better. As she pushed it away she saw that it was riddled with woodworm holes and had a deep split across the middle, then, looking closer, that it was a perfect example of an oak joint stool, hand-crafted, held together by wooden dowels with not a nail in sight. She had dealt with many, but never with one as obviously ancient as this. At a guess, she would put it at early sixteenth century.

Slater was watching her. "You know a lot, don't you," he said, and sighed. "When Poll said you was an antiques dealer I thought she meant—I dunno. Bits of china and things."

Doran didn't remember Poll saying anything about her profession. They must have been talking about her last night. "I have dealt in china, as well as furniture, but I'm not a specialist. I'm sorry to be so inquisitive, but I've got this awful curiosity about objects. Please forgive me."

"Like to see the galley? If you've finished your glass."

"Yes, please." The Bass had been good.

He trundled himself across the room to the door through which Polly had disappeared and gestured for Doran to go through it. The galley was another long, low room, with a wall once open like a balcony, now glazed in. The smell of river damp was strong here: Doran guessed the presence of rot. At one end a very small fire-place and a primitive stove indicated that any cooking was done there, but the importation of take-aways seemed more likely. There was neither gas nor electricity laid on, Slater said. Doran wondered once more how the place had escaped demolition or radical rebuilding. At the end opposite the cooking area was another door. Slater said, "Aloft," pointing upwards, and, "You'll excuse me if I don't take you further."

71

"Do tell me—were you ever a sailor?"

He smiled. "I been all sorts in my time, when I was a nipper. I got this—" he indicated his useless legs "—a good many years since. End of the sea for me."

"I'm sorry. It must be a terrible—handicap."

"I'm used to it. And I got Poll: she's a strong lass." Doran noted that his hands, like Polly's, were large, the hands of a man who had done manual work, now soft and clean-skinned with idleness.

"You're married—to a parson, Poll says."

She nodded. So they *had* been discussing her.

"Better be careful what I say, then."

"Oh, don't mind me, I'm not that sort of clergy wife— far from it."

"Got children, she says."

"Two. Would you like to see . . ." And she was producing snapshots, a young mother's inevitable luggage, from her handbag, and babbling on, as one did, about Armorel's beauty and placid temperament, Kit's cleverness and devotion to animals, all a mother's proud advertising spiel.

Slater looked at the photographs for a long time before handing them back. "They're very like you."

The words were coolly spoken, but the look said more. Doran, to her annoyance, found herself victim to her old enemy, a deep blush that spread from her forehead to her throat, a burning embarrassment that had been with her since school days.

Knowing that the blush was being noted, she hurried into chatter. "This house missed the Great Fire, of course? Yes, of course it did—it started at Pye Corner, didn't it. Or was it Pudding Lane? Just as well, or Paul's and the Tower might have gone. But I'm amazed this has survived—not just fire, people. Inspectors and things. And tourists."

"We've been lucky," he said. "They leave us pretty well alone. Frightened of the curse, maybe."

Doran leaped on this. "What curse?"

"Some old story. You don't want to bother with that."

Doran did very much want to bother with it, but she was beginning to feel guilty about staying so long. Obviously Slater had few visitors and was tiring, she guessed. She said, reluctantly enough, "I ought to go. Thank you for showing me your house. It's been fascinating. May I come back?"

"Any time," he said gravely. "Every day, if you like. If you want Polly, open the door and shout for her."

Poll reappeared, bade her uncle a casual farewell, and set off down the stairs to the street. Doran lingered. "Thank you," she said. "I *will* come back." She gave him her hand, which he took in both of his, and held.

"That's what Beauty said to the Beast," he said.

"She meant it, and so do I. And there's no comparison—you're not the Beast."

"No . . . Beauty?"

Feeling the blush rising again, she gently withdrew her hand and moved away. When she looked back he had drawn his chair to the fire again and sat, captive and helpless, his dark eyes fixed on her.

Polly seemed disinclined to talk, as was Doran. She tried. "You live in very different worlds, don't you—Copenhagen Court and—your home."

"You sayin' it's grotty? Well, right."

"No, I didn't mean . . ."

"Yeah, you did. See if I care. I was brought up in it, and so was me mum and me gran, and we'll go on till

73

there's none of us left. You think I'm muck, don't you—
but I done my bit."

None of this meant anything to Doran. She subsided
into her own confused thoughts. After a mad evening,
when she had made a bloody fool of herself, she had
spent a madder morning when she had made, if possible,
an even bloodier fool of the fantasy figure she had
become. Alice in Dockland. She felt strongly in favor of
signing the pledge, only where did one do such a thing
nowadays?

Her thoughts touched on home, and the discreet cluster
of bottles on their sideboard. Then, with a positive shock,
she realized that she had not thought of Rodney or Tiggy
once since breakfast.

And that, in a way, was the saddest thing of all.

"You shouldn't 'a done it, Mam," Howell said. He
said it in Welsh, which he and Gwenllian usually spoke
together. "You ought 'a known better."

"I *saw* it."

"You were nowhere near."

"I saw it all, what was happening, as if I was as near as
I am to you." They were talking at a singularly handsome
draw-leaf table in Abbot Owain's guest parlor, where
Howell had chosen to meet his mother rather than in the
local hotel: fewer temptations. Across the tabletop, pol-
ished for centuries by loving hands, she glared at him, in
his ill-fitting brown habit. He longed to stop the argument, to get on with his work of cataloguing Owain's
precious ecclesiastical belongings. He wished his mother
had not come rushing from London to confide in him,
taking his mind off his new-chosen way of life. He glared
back at her.

"You've been a fool, you and your visions. Interfering!"

74

"Would you have wanted her destroyed, my dear friend, as I could see was happening?"

"She's my friend too, lovely girl. And I don't have a lot of women friends. This way you could break her heart, kill her for all I know. And what about the other one, that Tiggy? You got any right to play God there?"

"I'll play God whenever I see it's needful. And talking about playing God, does your mate Owain know you still sneak off down to the pub for a quick one? Not very godly, that."

Howell buried his face in his hands. "Go on, put your oar in down here too. You'd like to see me back on the circuit, I bet, living it up so you could drop in and park yourself on me in between boyfriends."

"Whose boyfriends, yours or mine?" Gwenllian flashed at him.

"You know what I'm talking about, and let me tell you I don't hold with the way you've been managing your life—not decent at all. Look at this latest one; you've driven him off now."

"He was a swine, only fit to be driven off. I found that out in time, before we went abroad, insulting Dewi Sant."

"Maybe, but that doesn't give you the right to chuck him when you don't need his money."

"Who says I don't need it? He can take care of himself, that fat old bastard. His money was the only good thing about him."

"And where is he now, then?"

Gwenllian's mouth was mutinous. "I don't know; I can't see. I don't waste my gifts on such as him."

"You know that ring of yours is scratching this table, and it's a diamond. Owain'll have my blood if he sees a mark on it. Why don't you stop blathering and get back

75

to your pub? I think you've acted very wrong, and if I hear Doran's in any trouble, I shall go and sort it out for her, like I always have. Damn you and your visions, Mam, and God forgive me that I should say so."

Gwenllian pushed her chair back and ran out of the room, weeping noisily. It was the first serious quarrel she had had with her son for many years. An elderly brother, passing her on his way to the chapel, thought it was a sad pity the rules in this House were so lax, and resolved to light an extra candle for this poor old distressed female, who must be in serious spiritual trouble.

Then he smiled, as a boy's voice, pure as an angel's, floated across from the chapel, where a service had already begun. It was singing "Stabat Mater Dolorosa." The old man thought it sounded most suitable for the present moment.

But then he knew very little Latin.

Doran was getting used to phantom-ridden nights. This one was so disturbing that when she at last sank into a comfortable sleep, her usual hour of waking came and went. The room was bright with unfamiliar sunshine when she started awake to a replay of the previous morning—a strong hand violently agitating her shoulder. Poll's voice was saying something about people who never went to bed sober. But she'd had only hot milk the night before . . . Heavens! It was nine-thirty, even a little after.

"All right, all right." Doran was out of bed, scrabbling for her slippers. "And I went to bed perfectly sober—"

"Never mind that. The police is 'ere."

"*Who?*"

"The cops, the Bill, the Filth, what you like."

"What do they want?" She had found her dressing
76

gown, fortunately a decent woollen one with a high mandarin collar.

" 'Ow should I know? They're waitin'. I give 'em coffee."

"Good. I'll have a quick wash and be with them."

Carrying out a hurried toilette, Doran searched her memory for anything that could cause the police to call on her. A speeding offense on the drive from Kent? Illegal parking on the motorway? (No, she'd only stopped once at a service station.) Or—last and most horrible thought—something awful had happened to her family and they were here to break the news. Oh no, no.

Pale at this last possibility, she appeared in the salon (what else could one call it?) where two men were perched on huge overstuffed chairs looking about them, obviously uninterested in their coffee cups. Doran had had a good deal to do with the police in the past, but none quite like these. Both men were as informally dressed as men in their job could be expected to be. The younger, whom Doran rightly assumed to be the sergeant, wore his hair as close-cropped as an old-time convict's, a bomber jacket, and jeans. The elder appeared slightly more conventional, wore nonsexy spectacles, and spoke with one of those Edinburgh-flavored accents highly popular with television reporters.

Both leaped to their feet at Doran's entry and unashamedly stared. They had nice manners, she thought, but obviously had not been expecting anything like her, delicately pretty and clearly a lady.

"Mrs. Chelmarsh? Detective Inspector Moray, and this is Detective Sergeant Floyd." He presented ID cards. "Sorry to call on you so early, but we'd like a chat."

"Certainly." Doran chose a high-backed chair for moral support. She was aware of the sergeant's sharp eyes raking her from slippers to uncombed curls, and no doubt mentally removing the dressing gown. Her fears were subsiding: news of a family holocaust wouldn't be broken like this.

"Your maid tells me you are a friend of the owner of this flat, a Mr. Malcolm Grover?" His discreet phrasing gave him away: these two thought she was a high-class tart, and Mal her—whatever they call it, protector, perhaps. She started to blush from sheer indignation.

"Not a friend. I met him once, on Tuesday evening, when he took Mrs. Evans and me to dinner."

"Mrs. Evans." He was silently telling the sergeant what to write in his notebook. "And she would be . . . ?"

Another tart, you think, you nasty-minded copper? "Mrs. Gwenllian Evans is a friend of mine, an elderly lady. I came up from Kent on Monday to stay with her for a short holiday."

"Ah. Mphm. And whereabouts do you live in Kent, Mrs. Chelmarsh?"

"In Abbotsbourne, near Eastgate. My husband was vicar there until recently." She triumphed quietly at their obvious shock. The DI was uncertain of his next question.

"Ah, a vicar. I see." (Thinks now I'm some sort of *belle de jour*.) And have you heard from Mr. Grover since that evening?"

"No."

"Your telephone has been disconnected for part of the time, I believe?"

A nasty one. "Yes. I . . . needed a complete rest from, er, people."

A quick glance between the two. Now was the time to tell her. The sergeant spoke, a flattish South London voice. "Mr. Grover's car, registration PJF 2980L, was

78

found abandoned in a multistory car park in Lee Street, Wapping. It had been vandalized and all movable objects removed, except for a document in the glove compartment which gave us a Chelsea address for the owner. That address isn't where he lives now."

"The flat has been sold," put in the inspector, "and Mr. Grover has so far not been traced. The estate agent thinks he was going on holiday."

"Yes." The less Doran said, the better. Floyd went on to tell her that they had traced Grover's bank, solicitor, acquaintances in the Chelsea block where he had lived, and the man who acted as his chauffeur when required. No one could throw any light on his present whereabouts.

Doran marveled at their resourcefulness. She was less in favor of it when Moray proceeded to take her through the evening of Mal's birthday dinner, step by step, remorselessly. They went through every scrap of conversation Doran could remember until the earrings came up, when the DI became seriously investigatory. Had Doran ever seen the earrings? Had she the least idea what they were worth? Did Mrs. Evans mention any other items of jewelry given to her by Mr. Grover? What, exactly, had he said to Mrs. Evans when he accused her of selling them?

Doran's memory obliged with an accurate rendering. Moray asked, "You hadn't, of course, bought the earrings?"

"No. of course not! I used to deal in antiques, but I haven't for a long time. In any case, they're not the sort of thing I'd want."

"Aye, exactly. Now, Mrs. Chelmarsh, can you remember if Mr. Grover was wearing any jewelry—the sort of things some men wear, rings, cuff links, a tiepin?"

Doran thought. "I didn't study him all that carefully, but I think I'd have noticed. No."

"And did he wear a wristwatch?"

"I remember him glancing at it, once—I think the waiter was a bit slow bringing something to the table."

"Was it a valuable one—a Rolex, for instance?"

"I really didn't notice. But I should think it would be valuable, yes. Mr. Grover struck me as being the sort of man who wouldn't wear a cheap watch."

Moray sighed. Another Rolex mugging—only it seemed to be more than a mugging. His questions took a new turn. Was Doran sure that Mrs. Evans had returned to the flat that night? Would she have noticed if she had left it again? And, most important, where could Mrs. Evans be found now? They gathered from her maid that she had left two days earlier.

Doran experienced one of those blackouts of memory that come with an unexpected question pointedly asked. Now that she came to think of it, Gwenllian had said that she was going back to Wales, to somewhere near Howell. But pressed for the locality, all knowledge of Welsh place names deserted her. There was Cardiff and there was Swansea, otherwise there was a great green shape of mountains and rivers, quite unpronounceable even if she had known their names—but the space was blank. Hadn't Mrs. Evans's son said where this religious community was based? Moray inquired. Well, yes, she thought so, but had no idea where it was. Even to herself that sounded unlikely.

Did she think a map of Wales might help? Unfortunately, no. She was suffering from a bad case of witness's block, for which the printed page would hold no cure.

Moray, bristling with polite incredulity, told Floyd to

try the maid. The sergeant went to find her, rather to Doran's dismay: did the police think that confrontation would get at the truth from one of the two women? She and Moray sat in uncomfortable silence while Poll was fetched.

Poll arrived with a face of stubborn resentment. The opening dialogue was not promising.

"When did Mrs. Evans come here, Polly?" Moray asked.

"Name's Ms. 'Addock."

"I'm sorry, Ms. Haddock." Floyd didn't even try to suppress a grin. "When did Mrs. Evans come here first?"

"Dunno. Might be three weeks."

"And did she say where she had been living?"

"Didn't ask."

"Perhaps not, but it might just have come out in conversation."

Poll stared at him, flint-eyed, as communicative as a prison wall. Moray turned on his Nice Policeman act, often useful in coaxing information out of reluctant interviewees. His soft Scots accent was more noticeable; his brown eyes, behind their severe spectacles, acquired a melting warmth.

"Ms. Haddock, we do urgently need some information which Mrs. Evans may be able to give us. Not a lot of details, just a few wee facts. Now, it's obvious to me that you're a highly intelligent girl, and I feel sure you couldn't have worked for a lady without picking up some little . . . hint of where she might have come from?"

His hand went to his breast pocket, and lingered there as though he were about to produce something. Doran knew that the police were authorized to pay informers, or grasses or whatever, and saw the same speculation going through Poll's mind. She knew as surely as if she had

81

seen it that Poll had snooped in Gwenllian's belongings and would know, if anybody did, where she might have gone.

Sure enough, after a calculated long pause and an unconvincing performance of a person racking her memory, Poll said slowly, "There *was* something."

"Yes?"

"I seen a letter, come soon after she got 'ere. Noticed the postmark."

This, interpreted by Doran, meant that Poll had not only noted all postmarks on all letters, but had read any that had been left about. "Some saint, it was. Some Welsh name?"

"St. David's?" Moray prompted.

"That's right."

"Little place on the coast," said Floyd, "got a cathedral, though."

"Saint David's supposed to have been born there," added Doran.

"So." Moray sounded happier. "We have an address for Mrs. Evans. Good. Now, what we have to do is trace the community where her son's based. Can you help at all with that, Ms. Haddock?"

But Polly clearly felt she had said enough.

"Well." Moray rose, with relief. "I think we'd better get going. We could cover a lot of ground by midday. You won't be going too far if we need to interview you again?" he said to Doran. Don't leave town, in other words.

"Please," Doran said as they started for the door, "please . . ." She knew that Moray obviously, ridiculously, suspected Gwenllian of having made away with Mal, and struggled to defend her. But all that came out was, "Please give her my love if you find her."

* * *

But whatever Moray and Floyd were to find in Wales was pushed aside that night, when Mal himself was found in London. He was floating on the river near Barking Creek, and was horribly altered from the well-dressed diner who had flung out of the Trattoria San Paolo. There are river changes as well as sea changes.

Chapter 6

Doran wandered round the flat like a restless spirit. Good sense told her to follow her inclination and go home. She longed to talk to Rodney, who had been her other self for so long, to tell him of the odd and unpleasant things that had been happening, to hear his opinions and share in his mind again. With Gwenllian gone, there was no point in staying in London any longer. It had been a meaningless experiment which had brought her none of the excitement of change she had wanted—or thought she had wanted—apart from that one thrill of euphoria on her first evening, when she had seemed to see the river and the City brilliantly illuminated by fireworks.

But would Rodney, in his recent mood, want to know? His apathy towards her might be as bad as when she left him. He hadn't tried very hard to get in touch with her. Certainly she had blocked any approaches by instructing Polly to answer the telephone and say that she wasn't there. It had rung a few times, and her heart had leaped, but Polly had said nothing.

Nothing will come of nothing. How true, Lear. How flattening it would be to pour out her experiences to Rodney, and have them received with a murmured comment about early Norman architecture.

Then there was the shadow of Tiggy over Bell House. Was she still there, and even if not, what had happened while she had been?

And the children. Deliberately she kept them at the back of her mind, telling herself that Vi made the perfect substitute mother. No harm could come to them, surely, with a fond father, however abstracted, looking after them as well. All of which left Doran missing them desperately, half seeing them as ghosts may be half seen when one enters a haunted room. Kit and Armorel, Armorel and Kit, abandoned like latchkey children . . .

All of which made up her wavering mind. The weekend was coming, she had promised to go home, and she would go.

Yet there was a whole day left. She had seen nothing of the West End. Why not give herself a final treat, explore the shops, take a nostalgic look at Bond Street and Camden Passage, splash out on an expensive haircut and highlights, have a facial and an aromatherapy massage, finish up with a theatre or the Museum of London or dinner at a favorite secret restaurant off Knightsbridge, preceded by an enormous Pimm's?

Yes, that was the answer. Pleased with her own decisiveness, she dressed in clothes that would do for upmarket wear and set out, calling out to Polly that she would be away for the day.

No answer came. Doran looked in through the half-open kitchen door, to see Polly seated at the table, a bowl of soapy water beside her, intently cleaning something that shone.

"I shan't be back till tonight," Doran repeated. "Set the alarm, won't you."

The girl gave a perceptible start. "Right. Seeya."

So Polly cleaned the silver now and then, did she. And was shaken to be seen working. Well, well.

It may have been a breath of spring air from a blossoming tree in Island Gardens, or a breeze straight off the river, with a tang of spice cargoes and strange woods, that made Doran turn off the road that led to the taxi terminal and walk westward, as she and Polly had walked. She had no conscious thought about it.

This time she turned instinctively down the alley on the left. She was in cobbled Staple Lane, in front of the house of faded grandeur, without any conscious intention of being there. She went up the dark steps as if they were her own, knocked at the inner door, and went in without waiting for an answer.

He was not in his old place by the fire. Then she saw him through the window, sitting in the galley looking out over the river. He turned and smiled, beckoning her in. The galley was full of light and sun this morning; sunbeams danced on its walls.

"I knew you'd come back," he said.

"I told you I would, didn't I? But I started off to go into town and do the shops and galleries and things. I must be mad."

"That's the spring for you."

"Is it? I did wonder, just now, when I found myself here." She pulled up a chair and sat beside him at the open casement window. The river, below them, dimpled and sparkled, taking on the color of a cobalt sky as the sun came out fully; the breeze was soft and fresh, just fresh enough to encourage Doran to keep on the new caramel coat, which she knew suited her. It was an idyll, two people pleased with each other, in the setting of an Academy Exhibition picture.

86

The picture shattered. Something large and black and noisy erupted from the cooking end of the galley and propelled itself like a mad engine across the floor towards them. Doran gave a loud, irrepressible scream and sat trembling. The thing wasn't a machine; it was alive. Somewhere in that tousled mass of black, two eyes glinted wickedly. There was a slash of red among the black. She screamed again.

"Now, now, now," said Bill. "There, it's all right, he won't hurt you. He's only a chick."

"A—*chick*? I thought it was the Devil. What . . . what is it?" She shrank away, still shaking. Bill wheeled his chair up to the object, which was making squawking sounds. It shuffled up to him, and ceased to flutter as he stroked and murmured to it, seeming to tidy it up until it appeared as it was, a huge bird with fierce yellow eyes.

"I hope I'm not easily scared," Doran said, "but that thing frightened me out of my wits—I thought it was the Devil, truly. Sorry. How medieval can you get?"

"I'm sorry. I ought to have warned you. But you came in sudden, and it scared him. He really is a chick; he's only three months old."

"But what on earth is he?"

"A raven," said Bill simply, as one might say, "A sparrow."

"Like the ravens in the Tower?"

"He *is* from the Tower. One of the warders is a friend of mine, and he told me they'd got a bird hatched in February that was deformed. It's the foot, look." He lifted a crooked, twisted claw for her inspection. "They can't have birds on show to the public that's deformed, and the others would gang up on it. You know what birds are. So—" He drew his hand across his throat, expressively.

"The knacker's yard."

"Yeah. So I said I'd have it. Quiet place, this, nothing to upset him."

"Except me."

"He'll have to get used to people, won't he."

"Does the Queen know? There's the legend about the monarchy only lasting as long as the ravens are in the Tower—but perhaps it doesn't cover the Retired Hurt category."

"I expect they'll have told her. It's her bird, after all."

"Perhaps you'll get an OBE for befriending a member of the Royal household," Doran suggested facetiously. But Bill looked alarmed.

"No! People don't know where he is. I told my friend not to say."

"But why?"

"It wouldn't do." That was all he was going to say. Curious.

The great bird gave a muted squawk and looked pointedly at the table.

"Wants his dinner," Bill said affectionately. " 'Scuse me." He wheeled himself over to a cupboard by the fireplace and returned with what looked like a hamburger in an advanced state of decomposition. "Now," he said to the bird, "wait. Manners." It tilted its head but made no move towards the food.

"Right. Dinner, boy." The horny beak advanced and snapped up the hamburger, though Doran noticed that it made no attempt to bite the hand that fed it. When it had eaten, Bill stroked the red patch on its throat, which it seemed to enjoy. Doran asked what the color was.

"The young ones start off like that, then it goes. Pretty, ain't it. Here, Grim, show the lady your weskit."

"*What* did you call him—Grim?"

"Well, it sounds right for a raven—sort of name people expect. And it's a bit like Dickens's Grip."

That talented bird had been in Doran's mind, but she was amazed that this man should have even heard of it. He said, shyly, "I read a lot, you know," nodding towards a shelf of books among which there were some very ancient-looking leather spines.

"I never thought I'd meet a real Grip. Are you going to teach him to talk? Will he say, 'I'm a kettle' and 'Never say die'?"

Bill shook his head. "Bit too fancy. But I could teach him to say your name. Doran."

She felt the dreaded blush starting to creep up: his tone had been like a caress. Hastily she said, "I've got to go, or I'll never get to town today. Oh, what a mess I must look." Her handbag mirror showed her tousled hair and a shiny face.

"There's Poll's room up aloft, if you don't mind stairs."

So for the first time Doran saw, at the top of the rickety steps, more like a loft ladder, the rest of the building. It was all more or less what she expected—dark old paneling, much in need of repair, dust, cobwebs, and a pervading smell of damp and mice. She opened a latched door that must surely lead to "Poll's room," and paused, unbelieving.

The small room could have fitted into Copenhagen Court, within its degree. It was almost an elaborate mockery of the room she slept in there. The bed, which took up most of the space, was imitation Victorian brass, all white and gold, with knobs at the head and foot, covered by a duvet and valanced sheet, all roses—full and budded, pink, red, and white, a flowering riot. On the pillows sat a life-size nude baby doll, holding to its simpering pink cheek a garment presumably worn by Poll at night.

On the pine dressing table were ornamental trivia—figurines, cut-glass bottles and scent sprays, crystal animals—and a few bottles and boxes of expensive cosmetics. Doran wondered when and how Poll used these. On the walls were modern decorative plates of cutesy children and improbably nubile girls, all gold-edged, and one large poster of a current male pop star, wearing black leather and heavy makeup.

It was, Doran decided, a teenage whore's room.

Too stunned to do more than comb her hair at the gilt mirror, she made her way thoughtfully downstairs. On the tiny landing outside the galley were two doors, one, a quick glance showed her, a rough, minimal bathroom with a rusting old-style bath on claw feet, the other a bedroom smaller than Poll's, of monkish simplicity, little more than a cell. A prison cell, or an anchorite's cell. A crucifix above the bed heightened this impression. A curtained corner wardrobe held, presumably, all of Bill's clothes that he was not actually wearing. The room was light and clean, except for Grim's droppings and a musty feral smell which wild creatures in captivity seemed to produce.

In the galley a cup of instant coffee was waiting for Doran. It was not bad. Drinking it, she said, "It's an interesting house. How long did you say your family had lived here?"

"Don't think I did. But longer than most. I'm none too good at figures."

"Is there any more of it?"

"There's an attic, nothing in it, just odds and sods." He seemed slightly reluctant to talk about the house. "And a

90

very old bit, more like a cellar, under the stairs you come up by. Nothing there either, only kindling and clutter."

"Ah. Fascinating." Doran determined to get a look at this. "Your family must be pretty amazing, to have gone on so long. Were they very prolific?"

"Right. Children to each marriage. If the wife died in childbirth or the first lot of kids, they married again and got more. My dad did that, lost his first brood young, took another wife and had me and my sister when he was an old man. Lived to ninety-odd, he did." He sighed. "Never cared much for us, though. Pity the first lot didn't live, but they was gone. Lost."

"I suppose that's natural. The children of one's old age can't be a lot of fun. One's been through it all before, and babies do make a fearful noise and keep one awake. I was very lucky with my daughter; she was quite unbelievably good—in fact, we thought she was retarded. but I think she just enjoyed trailing her clouds of glory as long as possible and dreaming about cherubs . . ."

She saw that Bill was not listening to her: talking about his family had saddened him. She got up hastily.

"Lovely coffee, thank you. Now I've really got to go." She almost added, "Sorry," at the look on his face.

"All right. It was great, seeing you. Me and Grim needs company."

I'll bet you do, thought Doran, carefully negotiating the dark staircase. What a sad pair he and Grim made, the lonely crippled man and the wing-clipped young bird, roosting on a nest of what looked like rags in a corner, barred from the liberty of the Tower and the admiration of camera-clicking tourists. Presumably Bill got his vocabulary from Poll. the twentieth-century slang which didn't suit him. He should have worn doublet and hose and talked like someone out of *Richard III.*

91

At the foot of the stairs she noticed for the first time a short passage leading away from the house's entrance. Her insatiable curiosity led her to examine it. Yes, there was a door, of rough planks with a wooden doorknob, and no sign of a lock. Doran opened it.

And almost crashed headfirst onto the stone-flagged floor beneath her, down a short flight of dangerously worn steps. (This was the perfect house for breaking one's neck in, if one had a fancy that way.)

She was indeed in something old and very like a cellar. Lit only by a slit of a window, it was a room of stone, dominated by what had been an inglenook fireplace, once used for cooking. The remains of a chain hung from a hook—that would have held a cooking pot—and a primitive box grate was surrounded by the burn marks of dead fires. In a corner was a stack of wood and another of smokeless fuel. The air was dank, foul.

Doran was in all that remained of the original house that had stood on this site—when? Who was King then, a Plantagenet or a Tudor? How had the dwellers here been dressed, those folk shorter than today's people? There had been one King of six feet three who had been called a giant—who was that?

Rodney would have known.

But traveling to the West End by taxi, through an endless succession of traffic jams, she kept Rodney firmly out of her mind. He was not in this with her, and wouldn't be until the situation at home was cleared up. She was a true Gemini, but this time the Twin would have to stay out of it.

Yet, as she strolled through the luxurious halls of Harrods, holding tightly on to her bag and sniffing senuously the wafts of perfume, leather, coffee, rich materials, curry and garlic (the contribution of customers), a shade, not Rodney's, seemed to walk by her side. It was not unusual for her to summon up shades, people from history or favorite fiction, to talk to in her mind. Often they were more rewarding conversationally than the living. This phantom's hand was protectively beneath her elbow, and the soft bright lights gleamed on his curly grey hair. Why was she so drawn to grey-haired men, even shades? His tall figure and immaculate Greek profile would have been the cynosure of every female eye, if he had been visible.

But he was not. He was her old friend Dr. John Evelyn Thorndyke, summoned away from his patch in King's Bench Walk to investigate and discuss an interesting potential crime, with Doran, temporarily his acolyte. She had fallen under his spell long ago.

She toyed with costume jewelry, her ears alert for his pleasant voice.

"That was a remarkably strange room."

"Uncommonly."

"I should like to have lingered in it. But to my mind, the bedroom was even stranger. Every evidence of money, spent lavishly by a person with a somewhat vulgar taste. How do you suppose this money was obtained by Miss Haddock? Not from her wages, which one hardly supposes to be lavish, even in Copenhagen Court."

"I'm sure they're not. Five pounds an hour is the going rate, for her kind of work."

"Indeed. Fortunately I have no need of outside domestic services, my good Polton having so many skills—"

"Yes. Well, I'm glad Polton is still looking after you, Doctor, but to return to Poll Haddock. Obviously she's got a sideline going."

Obviously the good doctor was challenged. The sort of crimes he solved with such brilliance were more concerned with the reassembly of skeletons and the disposal of victims in amateur crematoria than with a cleaning lady's illegal hobbies. He said, uncertainly for him, "Pickpocketing? Uttering false notes?"

"I think she took things from her employers—those earrings, for instance. But that wouldn't be enough—there's got to be something else. Do you think she could be on the game?"

The noble brow was furrowed. He understood the meaning of the phrase, which had been current in his time, but that it should be uttered by a young lady of impeccable morals, with clerical connections . . . Doran saw his embarrassment.

"I'm sorry, I shouldn't have put it like that. I merely meant that some girls who are poorly paid sometimes . . . er, hang round the streets and pick up men."

"My dear young friend, say no more . . ."

They were in another taxi. The green stretches of Hyde Park were jeweled with daffodils and crocus. Outside Buckingham Palace the fountains played and a flag fluttered over the royal home.

"What about the uncle?" Doran asked. "None of this money gets spent on him. What does he think about it?"

"I doubt if he even knows. I doubt, further, whether he has ever seen his niece's room as it now is. The stairs are steep, and he has no need to go up them."

"No. That's true. Does she ever take him outside, even? Could that wheelchair be used in the street? What an awful life. Spending every day, every hour, in those rooms. Most people would go barking mad. It's no better than a prison sentence. But he seems so calm, so resigned."

"There are prisoners who feel they have deserved their sentence," Thorndyke said enigmatically. "Possibly Mr. Slater is one."

He might have added, "With that thought I leave you," for, while she pondered the remark, the cab had arrived at the Piccadilly end of Bond Street, and she was paying the driver. Her companion had faded away as such shades did, to be replaced by the Prince Regent, laying a bet with a crony about the number of cats they would meet on that side of the street.

But how many cats were they likely to meet there? One would be a crowd in today's conditions . . . With such dreamy reflections, Doran made her way north, past the chemist's where Emma Hamilton had no doubt bought remedies for the ailments caused by too much porter, poor dear.

Musing on beauty and its impermanence, she happened to find herself at the entrance to one of the houses that ruled that world internationally. Suddenly all cultural plans for her day vanished. She would not go to an art exhibition on the South Bank; she would simply go through this inviting automatic door and be transformed. It wouldn't take long, just for a facial.

And so, four hours later, she emerged into Bond Street feeling a goddess. Her hair tossed brightly in apparently windblown charm which famous fingers had snipped and shaped; her face was a warm pearl, as clean as though the oyster had just disgorged it. Her nails were ten smaller pearls, almost colorless but gleaming with life. Her body tingled from the masseuse's hands, relaxed to cloudlike airiness from the tip-up chair in the room colored like the first blush of dawn.

Her checkbook was lighter of a sum that, Doran felt, would have just about paid for a Society wedding. Who cared? She smelt wonderful, too, and a phial of *Jeunesse Dorée* was in her carrier bag.

It was shortly joined there by a delicious silky clinging dress in a pale apricot, a color Rodney had once admired, and a pair of earrings of crystal, in mock-Victorian pinchback settings, set with tiny many-colored jewels, which magically reflected whatever she wore: she'd tried them against blue, gold, rose, and deep amber, watching with delight as they turned from one jewel into another.

By now, having reversed her tracks, she had reached Piccadilly. A gentle chiming came from Fortnum and Mason's clock, and the two little figures in Georgian footmen's dress came out and gave each other their formal greeting before retiring. Half past six.

Even on this self-indulgent, spendthrift day Doran's intentions didn't include dinner at the Ritz. She found a small, modest French restaurant that did pretheatre meals, and had a small, modest meal.

Dr. Thorndyke, who had made himself scarce at the great beautician's where he would have been decidedly uncomfortable, quietly slid into a chair beside her.

"Some fortunate swain is going to be charmed by a rare sight of beauty adorned," he observed. He was not at his best in the world of women and tended to become flowery.

"There isn't a swain," Doran replied swiftly. Thorndyke scrutinized her over the rim of the pretty Bohemian wineglass he had taken up. It was empty, as the waiter did not observe his presence.

On safe ground, he said, "I am still very exercised by the room in the basement of Slater's house. To my mind it could be a rare survival of a medieval building. All it lacks is a body: I should expect a few remains in such a place. And it would *so* delight Polton: Polton really enjoys an exhumation."

"I agree it would be interesting, but I'm not going to ask Mr. Slater to have his basement dug over just to gratify Polton."

The little manservant with the crinkly smile immediately materialized in another chair, rubbing his hands in anticipation and looking eagerly from one to the other of them.

Doran immediately switched off. She was not going to have her delicious sole *bonne femme* spoiled by phantasms who were after all only personifications of her own subconscious mind. Nonsense. This was her day; she would live it out to the full.

She was back at Copenhagen Court by eight o'clock, just in time, she thought, to stretch out luxuriously on her special sofa and watch a television program she rather liked, one of the cops-with-brains genre. She was tired, but pleasantly so, and the hall mirror, reproduction American crowned by an eagle on rocks, certainly showed a very different creature from the one who had gone out that morning.

But the hall also contained the answering machine, where a tiny red light shone. There had been a message—damn. Someone breaking her mood.

She pressed the playback switch. The voice was pleasant, familiar Scottish: the voice of Chief Inspector Moray, politely asking her to ring his extension when she came in. He had tried her several times, but her maid had not appeared to understand the message.

Poll being bloody-minded. Damn again. She called the number. Moray himself answered.

"Sorry to trouble you at this time of the evening, madam, but something a bit urgent's come up." She

97

listened, hardly taking in what he told her, that a body had been washed up early that morning which the police had reason to believe was that of Mr. Malcolm Grover. They would like her to come and identify it.

"But—I hardly knew him. I only met him once. Surely there must be someone else . . ."

"No next of kin to be found. And there are—difficulties—with the few people who had met him."

Naturally. Like nobody wants to be the first to offer for a nasty job. But curiosity, and a mixture of other feelings, propelled Doran into agreeing. Moray would collect her in half an hour or so and take her to the mortuary.

It was something to have a man as audience for her glorified appearance, something else that the man was Detective Inspector Moray, whose eyes were accustomed to looking on all sorts and conditions of women, and not accustomed to expressing pleasure at the way they looked. Sitting opposite him in the featureless office where uniformed and plainclothes people worked or came in and out, Doran felt she might as well have been wearing a bag over her head.

His manner, she thought, was just a shade colder than it had been before. Probably the other acquaintances of Malcolm, the banker, the solicitor, and the chauffeur, were all perfectly available; he had chosen her because of a lurking suspicion that she had had something to do with the death.

Which was true. The waiters at the San Paulo had testified to the scene over dinner, to the man's fury and the shocked reaction of the women, and the fact that they and the man had left separately, but they couldn't say that they might have met up again outside.

A common story, perhaps—a confrontation, a renewal of the quarrel. They could have been standing danger-

98

ously near the river's edge; the fiery little Welshwoman could have struck out at the half-drunk Grover, who would have toppled into the river . . . It was all speculative, but not to be dismissed.

"I'm sorry to have to ask you to do this, Mrs. Chelmarsh," Moray said. "Not a pleasant job. But someone has to do it."

"That's all right. I had dinner early, in town," Doran said cheerfully, aware of slight outrage on Moray's part. Good. "And I have seen quite a few corpses, in my time."

"Really? Then we'd better get on with it."

The two of them and Floyd sat in his car in silence, as it traveled swiftly through quiet evening streets, going westerly. Familiar shapes began to appear. Doran wondered where they were going—a hospital, or some disused building used as a mortuary?

In spite of her airy words to Moray, she was dreading the experience before her. She looked at her watch. In an hour it should all be over, and she could go back to Copenhagen Court and try on the apricot dress, with a touch of *Jeunesse Dorée* for sheer luxury.

The car turned left and began to seek out a parking spot.

"But . . ." began Doran.

They were at the foot of Tower Bridge. Moray had stopped the car, opened the door for Doran, and was leading her unmistakably towards one of Horace Jones's great iron-hearted Gothic pillars. She followed him down a few steps and through a menacing metal door.

"Here we are. This is where bodies found in the river are brought."

One had seen it all before, of course, in television mock-ups. The shrouded form on the table or in the drawer, the slow lifting of the covering sheet from the

99

face, then the look of frozen grief or whatever emotion was appropriate from the witness. So far it was routine. Doran was acutely aware of Moray watching her keenly without seeming to look at her, and of Floyd staring at her openly. She could feel the tension in her muscles and the tautness in her face.

Nothing had prepared her for the sight revealed by the removal of the sheet. That bloated horror had surely never been a face—no face could be that indescribable color, the features . . .

What features? A wave of horror surged over Doran. Surely fish didn't abound in this stretch of the Thames, and yet—the face was not all there. A loathsome glimpse of swollen nudity, scarred and bruised, showed below it, and the distorted ruin of what had been a shoulder.

Fighting surge after surge of nausea, she forced herself to look at the thing, keep her mind on it. There was something—the reddish hair, now dark with water, and the way it grew in tufts. Her hand to her mouth, she signaled to them to cover the body.

Moray knew all about the way witnesses reacted to drowned corpses. Very quickly he steered Doran to the adjacent bathroom, and left her there.

Floyd said, "Seen plenty of 'em, has she." He snorted.

"Not all like this one. Very nasty."

When Doran returned, the mortuary attendant had removed the body. A chair was waiting for her, and a glass of brandy. Moray, to her surprise, offered her a cigarette, and even more to her surprise, she took it. Damn the government health warnings, at a moment like this.

The ministrations of Bond Street's beauticians might never have taken place. "The Fall of the House of Usher," Doran had said to her spectral reflection in the mirror. Even Poe couldn't have improved on it. She drank the brandy at one swallow, wishing very much that she had a warm, sympathetic masculine hand to hold. Preferably Rodney's.

At least Moray was kinder now. He apologized again, sounding sincere, for exposing her to such a sight.

"But it was necessary—we have to know who he is. I suppose you didn't recognize him?"

"Hardly. But I did notice one thing, the hair." She described the way it had appeared in life. "And he combed the long pieces from one side across the top, to disguise the fact that he was bald."

Floyd scribbled. The attendant reappeared and held a whispered conversation with Moray before disappearing again, doubtless to try the effect of such a coiffure on his subject. (Didn't they call them subjects?)

"Do you recognize this as belonging to Mr. Grover?" Moray was showing her a small chamois purse, attached to a soft elastic belt, and a handful of folded five-pound notes. All had obviously been in the water and were soggy with damp.

"No. It looks like the sort of thing people wear round their waists so as not to get robbed abroad. Or anywhere, really."

"Exactly. My mother used to say to me, 'Never let yourself be caught away from home without a five-pound note, Jamie. It'll get you a taxi at the least.' " All this was said in a warm, cozy Scots accent, designed to soothe. "I'd say this was worn on the same principle."

"I'm sure it was just the kind of thing . . . Mr. Grover would wear. But I can't possibly identify it."

"He'd been stripped of his top clothes," Floyd put in. "Turned up just in his shirt and underpants. This was

101

next to his skin. What was he wearing, that you could see?"

"Er. A very expensive overcoat—something like mohair, I don't know what it's called. It was a sort of darkish brown. And a dark suit—again I can't say what it was. Only I got the impression of wealth, as though everything he wore had cost a lost of money."

"Shirt and pants certainly did," said Floyd. "Didn't believe in chain stores, our Mr. Grover."

"If we could only get hold of Mrs. Evans," Moray said wistfully. "We never did make it to Wales. There're a lot of things we'd like to ask her. Well, we'd best be on our way. Oh, Mrs. Chelmarsh, did I tell you—the police doctor's looked at him, and it wasn't the water that killed him. His neck was broken."

"Oh no!"

"Anything else will show up at the autopsy, when they've sorted out the damage done by boats and underwater objects. Then we'll be a bit nearer to knowing what happened. Mind the steps, they're a wee bit slippy."

In the mock-Gothic porch of a terrace house on the outskirts of St. David's stood Howell, shifting from one sandaled foot to the other. It was raining, very wet Welsh rain, and damp was seeping between the hood of his cassock and his neck. He mostly kept the hood down because the appearance of a cowled head frightened people; they said it made them think of ghosts.

The door was opened by a lady who, though her origins were in Lancashire, found exile in Wales no hardship. There was a comfortable living to be made by keeping a guesthouse in a place where hardy people came to stay, whatever the weather. She was not particularly fond of the native Welsh, a feeling that was reciprocated.

One glance at the brown habit placed her caller neatly. One of *those*. With a collecting box, most likely.

"Good evening," said Howell politely. "I wonder if you have a Mrs. Evans staying with you?"

"Well. I did have, but she's left."

"Oh dear. Did she say where she was going?"

"No. And I didn't ask. None of my business."

Howell knew from the tone of the reply that Gwenllian and her landlady had taken an instant strong dislike to each other. It happened, and he knew better than to inquire further. If Gwenllian wanted to hide, there was no more he could do about it. He said a polite thank you and good evening, and trailed off into the night, watched suspiciously by the guesthouse's owner, who kept a few hens round the back.

He wished earnestly that he were not dressed like a mendicant friar in a comic opera. His feet were cold, he could feel a sneeze coming on, he hated having the use of his car restricted.

He wished passionately that Doran hadn't embarked on this blasted silly adventure, which would see them all in a lot of trouble before it was over.

Chapter 7

If this was adventure, you could keep it, and if it was the romance of detection, you could keep it as well. Doran savagely undressed and threw her clothes about the bathroom, running the hot water as though she were flooding an enemy stronghold.

Everything she had worn that evening, even her skin, smelt of the place of death where she had been. The shapeless parody of a face haunted her mind—no bath essence would wash *that* out. She went back into her room for cleansing cream, anything to purify her body from the taint that clung to it.

The cream was already packed. Enough was enough. Tomorrow she would go back home, as she had promised, and stay there. There would be time to telephone when she had had the very necessary bath. Her luggage was light, fortunately, half of it packed already.

With the cream, she was back in the bathroom when a sound made her freeze. Somewhere in the flat a door had opened. Gwenllian back? Or—someone who ought not to be here?

But when she went out to face whoever it was, she saw nothing worse than Poll, coming out of the master bedroom.

"Poll—what on earth are you doing here?"

"Sorry. Did I scare you?"

"Yes, you did. Now, what's this about?"

Poll's manner was muted, lacking its usual sullen insolence, and she looked even paler than usual. "Well, just before me usual time for goin' 'ome, I started to feel rough."

"What sort of rough?"

"*You* know. Pains and a sorta sick 'eadache. I took some of me pills and I got sleepy. So I 'ad a lie-down, and next thing I knew, I'd been asleep coupla hours. Only just got up."

She did indeed look ill. Doran said more kindly, "Well, you can stay the night if you like. I'll be going home in the morning, so you won't have any more to do here; you can just clear up and go off in your own time."

Poll looked dubious. "What abaht me wages? I was to get 'em end of every week."

"Well, I'm afraid you won't be getting them from me, because Mr. Grover's your employer. At least he was, but he's dead—I've just been identifying his body."

Poll was even paler. "Where? What 'appened?"

"He was found in the river. He'd been robbed and . . . Never mind. But the police do know about him, and I expect they can get his solicitor or someone to pay you."

"They better 'ad."

"They will. They've been marvelous, getting so much information already. Now, I'm going to have a very long bath, so you can go back to bed, and I hope you feel better in the morning."

"Yeah. Thanks."

The bathroom door shut behind Doran.

But Poll didn't go back to bed. When she heard the gentle roar of the bathwater, and a thread of classical music from Doran's transistor, she went softly and silently to the two pieces of luggage. They were invitingly open, but there was no need for Poll to go through them. She had already searched Doran's drawers and wardrobe in the two hours since she had come back, expecting Doran to be home late from town.

Now, in her comfortably compressible bag on the floor, were all the choicest bits of jewelry, several of the least worn and prettiest articles of lingerie, an elegant silk jersey dress which could be packed as small as a handkerchief, and several pairs of tights.

The perfume bottles were no use; they'd been opened. But she cast a longing look at the *Jeunesse Dorée*, rejecting it with difficulty: too obvious. About the other items, she could lie stonily if ever questioned by the police. But somehow she didn't think she would be—she had Doran pigeonholed as a soft touch, somebody who wouldn't complain in case it started trouble.

Then, her loot packed in her carrier bag, she waited for Doran's return from the bathroom.

The cleansing ritual proved soothing, a cassette of *Death and the Maiden* even more so. Romantic melancholy of Schubert's sort carried no suggestion of Tower Bridge mortuary. As an extra precaution, Doran took a sleeping pill.

She was surprised when Poll appeared in her bedroom with a tray.

"Thought yer'd like a nightcap, after all that at the morgue. Scotch wiv water, right?"

"Right. You're very kind, Poll."

That one should ever say such a thing, to Poll of all people. But perhaps malaise calmed her—she certainly seemed different tonight. Doran drank her nightcap, aware from the taste that Poll had got hold of one of the inferior bottles of Scotch. But never mind, it worked.

Strange, vivid, disturbing dreams came to her that night. Armorel, crying for once, reaching up for an embrace. Kit, on the verge of tears, as he became when animal cruelty was in question, protesting over and over. "But it needs exercise!" Rodney, dressed again as Jack Point, reciting, "Oh, woe is me, I rather think!" And a nightmare figure, nobody she knew, a witch or demon, which seemed to grow larger and smaller by turns, menacing them all. A creature of indescribable evil, a terror-bringer.

And then a warm ray of sunlight touched Doran's eyes, as with unspeakable relief she woke from the phantasmagoria. For a long moment she lay still, slowly savoring the knowledge that all the horrors had been dreams.

A nasty sulfurous taste was in her mouth, and a sharp ache beat inside her head. She might have had a heavy session at a nightclub with such a hangover, and all for one not very nice nightcap.

But thank God it was morning, and she was going home, home to all those who had been weeping and calling her name, and who would be their perfectly normal selves when she saw them again. It was going to be a lovely day, by the strength of the sun: good. A pleasant drive, on the road before any hopeful weekenders started for the coast.

She reached for her watch from the bedside table, then froze in unbelief.

It was twelve o'clock. Noon.

"Oh God, don't let them think I'm not coming." Had she telephoned last night, as she meant to do? Impossible to remember. What a strange sleep that had been, apart from the dreams—unconsciousness for—what? thirteen hours, perhaps more. She, who had a built-in alarm clock

107

that had started ticking at Kit's birth. There was something horribly unnatural about all this.

Her guess was accurate. As soon as Poll judged her asleep the previous night, she had disconnected all the telephones but the one in the kitchen, the farthest room from Doran's. Then she had dialed the number.

"Is that the Reverend Chelmarsh? Oh. Yer don't know me; I'm the maid where she was stayin' in London. That's right. Well, I thought I better tell yer. She said she was goin' 'ome tomorrow, Sat'day. Then she went out last night, took all her bags, and never come back. I thought I better say, in case you was wonderin'. No, she wasn't on her own. She went wiv a feller. I dunno what he was called—somebody she picked . . . met in town, could be. They could've come down to Kent, I wouldn't know. None of my business. Only I 'ad to tell yer. Yeah, if I 'ear anything, I'll call yer. Good night."

Rodney listened to the story with shock, disbelief, then, against all reason, a horrified belief. Doran had avoided getting in touch with him for days. She was deeply offended by Tiggy's arrival, he knew. And perhaps there had been something else—some*one* else.

Doran, to leave him like that. It was late at night and he was stupid with sleep, poleaxed by what the kind, well-meaning girl had told him, shaken with grief and anger. He swept the telephone aside and sat slumped, his head on his arms.

So Vi found him when, roused by the bell, she had come out of her room. She touched his shoulder gently, saying, "Go back to bed, Mr. Rodney. Whatever it is, it'll seem better in the morning."

But it didn't. By morning he was distraught. Ignoring Vi's protests, unshaven and breakfastless, he got out the

108

car. They were a two-car family and his was the older one, a graceful Citroën that had seen better days but wasn't due for retirement. It had never let him down— until this morning.

Repeatedly he tried the ignition, looked under the bonnet—which told him nothing, as he knew absolutely nothing about cars except how to drive them at a moderate speed—used words not normally heard from him, and even resorted to kicking the car, an infallible remedy that seemed to have lost its power.

All this time he had been watched by a silent, frightened Kit. He had never seen his father in such a state. He felt, though nothing had been said, that it was somehow connected with danger to his mother, and his world trembled.

Timidly he said, "Shall I go to the garage for you, Daddy? They might start it for you. Or they might lend you another car."

Rodney drew his hand across his oil-streaked face, making it even dirtier. "Brilliant idea, Kit. Why didn't I think of that earlier? Because I'm a fool, that's why. Come on, we'll both go."

Kit brightened up, cheered at being able to help. They set off into Abbotsbourne.

But Jack at the garage, a friendly man who had often helped out the unmechanical family, had no comfort to offer. "If she won't start, she won't start, Mr. Rodney—I did warn you last time. She's an old lady—when did she have her last MOT?"

"I haven't the slightest idea."

"Well, anyway, even if I got her going, I wouldn't advise you to drive to London in her, not on a Saturday morning, with the sun out."

Kit said, "But you do have another car, don't you—the one you lend sometimes."

"Well, yes, I do, Kit, but it's out. Lent it to a man over at Elvesham for the weekend." Rodney's despairing face moved him to add, "I'll tell you what, though. If I get Neil to take over for a bit, I could drive you to Barminster and you could get the train."

Rodney thought. It would be tedious, but it was the only solution. Reluctantly he agreed.

Kit pulled at his sleeve. "Daddy. Hadn't you better wash your face? You look a bit—well . . ."

Rodney needed no mirror to confirm his son's doubt about his appearance. Refusing Jack's offer of the staff washroom, he set off for home, Kit trotting gamely at his side. At Bell House he washed, changed out of the jeans and old shirt he had been wearing, and, at Vi's suggestion, supplied himself with money and his checkbook.

He didn't tell Vi about the unnerving telephone message. To voice it would make it even more real. His sense of evil, which had always been strong, was overwhelming, and he would not willingly involve anyone else in it.

She had listened-in to it anyway.

Doran had always defended herself, if only in her own mind, against charges of impulsive flightiness by recalling Johnson's remark about a female similarly accused: something to the effect that *Sir, the woman has a bottom of good sense.* Then, aware of Boswell's incipient titters, he added sternly, *The woman is fundamentally sensible.*

She now proved her own worthiness of the description

110

by making a pot of strong tea and taking two Alka Seltzers with it.

Poll had obviously been behind the time lapse: it wasn't difficult to connect her with the unpleasant taste of the nightcap. She had slipped Doran a Mickey Finn, for her own purposes. What they were was not beyond speculation, and was confirmed when Doran unpacked her two cases. She knew every possession she had brought to London with her. Quite a few of them were missing. And the top of the *Jeunesse Dorée* had been loosened—Poll hadn't been able to resist a dab or two of it.

The tea was clearing her mind; the Lexicographer would have approved of that. Her memory of the previous night was beginning to come back, and there was not the faintest echo in it of a familiar voice. Now she was quite sure she hadn't telephoned Bell House.

So they were not expecting her definitely today. That was one relief: she had time to iron it all out. And the first thing she would do, now that her anger was rising to a healthy glow, would be to confront the thief. It was high time Poll Haddock got her comeuppance.

This time, arriving at the old house, she charged up the stairs as though she lived there, flung open the door, and confronted not Poll, but Bill Slater.

He was in his old place by the fire, which was unlit. The room smelt stale, shut up.

When he saw her his face was suddenly illumined, as if torchlight had been thrown on it. He put out his hand towards her, saying, "Doran." The bird was crouched in its corner, unmoving. Suddenly she heard Kit's dream-voice, lamenting, "It doesn't get enough exercise!"

She took the cold hand, warming it in both her own.

111

"What's the matter? Are you on your own? Where's Poll?"

"Not back—yet."

"Excuse me." She ran up to the bedroom. There it was, in all its gaudy splendour, the bed made and no sign of occupation. A quick glance round showed no sign of the missing objects. But her anger now was not for them.

"She didn't come home last night," she said to Bill downstairs.

"No. Must've gone off somewhere."

"Yes, and I can guess where—to whatever fence she uses."

"Fence? Oh. Has she been at it again?"

"Yes, if you mean what I think you mean. Quite a bit—some jewelry included. Where does she go?"

Bill looked unhappy. "She don't tell me."

"But you know, don't you? Come on, tell, she's got to be stopped."

"You don't understand."

"Possibly, but Poll doesn't need understanding; she needs catching. Now, where is she?"

Reluctantly, not looking at Doran, he said, "Brighton."

"Oh indeed." London-by-the-sea, happy home of dedicated criminals as well as of innocent lovers of its intoxicating air, its Pavilion, its Downs, the merry raffishness that had somehow outlived the Prince Regent. Doran imagined a slender silver necklace of linked Cupids of which she was particularly fond on sale in the Lanes, and her new lingerie next to a chair full of Edwardian lace. Well, never mind that now.

"What did she leave you to eat—and drink?" she asked, eyeing a glass of water by Bill's side.

"Well. Bit of cold ham. And some milk, but it's gone off. Probably didn't expect to be away so long."

"Haven't you anybody who runs errands? Someone who looks in and asks if you want anything?"

He shook his head. "I'm all right."

"You look it, I must say, exactly like the Spirit of Christmas. And what about *him*?"

The raven looked smaller than before, a mere heap of feathers from which the iridescent sheen seemed to have faded. The gold eyes that had opened when Doran entered were shut again. Bill reached down and touched the crested head.

"I'm a bit worried about him. But it's not Poll's fault ..."

"It can be the governor of the Tower's fault, for all I know. I'm sorry, I don't mean to snap. Now, excuse me if I seem to pry."

Which she did, looking into the small, dark, and insecty cupboard in the galley and the larger but empty one by the fireplace, searching a small concealed drawer which proved to have old broken cutlery in it, inspecting with horror the contents of a bucket full of scraps of old food. To her relief she saw a roll of black dustbin bags where nobody could have expected to find them. She waved them at Bill.

"Where do these go—when they're full, I mean?"

"Outside the front door, for the dustmen."

"Right. I'll fill one and take it out. I'm going out myself now. Not for long—twenty minutes, possibly. Don't worry, I'll be back."

In fact, she was away rather longer, for the district was poor in shops. At last she found a small but well-stocked supermarket which was doing a lively Saturday trade. On the way to it was a branch of her bank with a cash dispenser. Normally she would have hesitated to use one of these in London, with mugging in mind, but today her

113

adrenaline was high. She picked a loose brick off a low garden wall and held it conspicuously in one hand, while conducting the transaction.

When she returned to the old house she was carrying two outsize plastic bags. Bill, who had been brooding in his chair, stirred at her entrance and watched incredulously as she unpacked them and piled their contents on the joint stool and a rickety old table.

There was a sliced whole-meal loaf, a pound of Irish butter, sugar, tea, coffee, and several cartons of milk. Frozen packs contained meat, fish, and small, pretty bouquets of vegetables. A generous selection of French and English cheeses spread a double fan of color; bottles of dessert fancies jostled a brown-topped apple pie and its attendant cream. Two bunches of grapes, one white, one purple, spilled ripe fruits onto the dirty floor. Bars of chocolate glittered here and there.

The cornucopia emptied, Doran went downstairs and returned with an oval plastic box. "Cold box," she explained. "For picnics. One freezes the units inside and it serves as a refrigerator, which this horrible place hasn't got. How do I freeze them, you ask? I go to a pub and borrow their fridge. They'll love it, you'll see. It's amazing how Christian people get when it comes to feeding the needy, especially with something they haven't paid for themselves."

Bill's wondering smile turned to laughter. She hadn't known he could laugh, and like that.

"I don't believe you're real," he gasped. "I don't believe this is true. You an angel, or what?"

"No. I'm a figment of Dickens's imagination, left over from Christmas, and so are you, and so is he—"

"Grim?"

"No! I won't have him called by that silly name. Grip

114

was good enough for Dickens and it's good enough for us. Grip? Look, he knows his name."

The bird had moved, was watching her. She unwrapped one of the plastic boxes and began to spread the contents on a sheet of paper. They were pieces of beef, cut up bite-size; any chef would have recognized them as best sirloin steak. Doran, with coaxing clucks and coos, spread the paper on the floor. Grip uncoiled himself, hopped as well as he could towards the meat, then with swift, greedy pecks began to eat.

"Cor," said Bill.

The galley was not a promising area in which to produce a *cordon bleu* meal. A small iron grate, caked with grease, had a bar above that let down, perhaps a grill or a pan rest, and another that let down in front. There was no oven.

A cupboard held three pans which were not and never had been nonstick, bearing stains and traces of their former contents. There was a cracked old butler's sink, a cold tap above it, and (remarkable) a tin of abrasive for scrubbing pans. Doran scrubbed the three until one could see what they were made of. Her pearly nail varnish began to crack and peel.

There was no fire, but crumpled paper, matches, and fuel from the sinister cellar provided one. Bill stared as she emerged from below with the fuel, then shook his head as one growing used to miracles. And Doran, a mediocre cook even with reasonable equipment, but inspired by she knew not what, produced a meal of fillet steak almost perfectly done, fresh baby sprouts with the cross properly cut on the base, golden corn on the cob, and a piece of fried Brie to accord with her own vegetarian tastes, accompanied by gooseberry jam.

Bill said something under his breath which she couldn't hear, but caught the word *Dominus* and knew that it was a Latin Grace before Meat. They both ate hungrily: Doran had had no breakfast. Then she brought in imported strawberries, served in cracked saucers, and a pottle of cream.

Bill could not finish his. He pushed away his saucer and sat looking at her as though she were an unearthly visitant who would not stay long and must be memorized.

"I must," she said, having finished every last one of her own strawberries, "tell you something that's on my mind. I know that you were starving and you're glad to have had a meal. So am I—I was starving too. But I'm not quite happy because I've made you feel like an object of charity, isn't that so?"

Bill nodded.

"Right. Well, let me tell you that that meal, rough as it was (and it *was* rough), was the only thing that's made me happy since I came up to London on Monday— except a bit of shopping, and that was self-gratification, not real happiness. I've had a bloody awful week. I won't tell you about it, but believe me, it was a shocker. Any week that ends in a mortuary can't be good news."

"A mortuary? Why? Who . . ."

"Never mind. The point is that I've done what I wanted to do. I've fed you and I've fed Grip, and because in some way I care about you both, I feel happy—you've done me a service by being my guests, as it were. And now we're going to have some of your instant coffee and a Benedictine. I thought somehow you'd like a Benedictine."

"I've never had any before," Bill said after a sip. "It's lovely. It's all lovely."

"Yes, it is. It's like waking up from a nightmare and going straight into a beautiful dream."

The late afternoon light was darkening, a few lights bobbing up on the river. Doran left her chair and went to sit on the joint stool at Bill's side, her cheek against his shoulder. He smiled down at her, took her greasy hand, scorched where a coal had burnt her palm, and kissed it.

Rodney had spent one of the most wretched days of his life. A slow train, a long taxi queue, a driver who, whatever the scope of his professional knowledge, managed somehow not to include Copenhagen Court in it, and at the end of the journey—nothing.

The flat was impregnable, silent. He applied at all the doors in that wing of the building, in vain. Some tenants were out—it was Saturday afternoon—the others were not prepared to admit a strange man, whoever he said he was.

The caretaker, ultimately found in a basement flat, was watching football with his feet up and a row of cans of lager at his side. He was not pleased to see Rodney and deeply suspicious of his motives. The flat belonged to a Mr. Grover and no, he didn't know where to get hold of him. There *had* been an old lady there—yes, Welsh by the way she talked—but he'd only spoken to her once or twice. He hadn't seen any young one, but it wasn't his business who came and went, so long as they behaved.

All the time he reluctantly answered Rodney's questions, his eyes were upon the television screen, where Arsenal were doing something lethal to Liverpool. No, he couldn't possibly let Rodney into the flat—strictly against rules, more'n his job was worth. He suggested Rodney come back in the morning—or maybe after the

117

weekend. His attention returned to the screen, as he joined in the supporters' cries of "Show 'im the card!" "Kick 'im!" "Get the bastard off!" and other, less seemly suggestions.

Rodney, sharing the feelings of the unpopular football player, left. By now he was tired, frustrated, and worried out of his mind. He could think of nobody to ask, nothing useful to do. At last, clinging to an increasingly faint hope that Doran might suddenly appear, he decided to stay in London.

On the way he had seen a large, opulent hotel near Tower Bridge. He found a taxi, booked in at the hotel, which found him a rather soulless room with a restricted view, then grew desperate with boredom and went to the nearest cinema.

His notion of a good film was something in black and white made before World War II. He had thought of himself as broad-minded, but was severely shaken by what he was seeing on this screen. He left abruptly, returned to the hotel, and remembered little of that night, and its dreams of fruitlessly searching for his lost wife and whoever had told him that lie—truth?—about her.

In the monastery outside St. David's, Howell took to his bed with a feverish cold. The bed was narrow and hard, the prospect of his bare cell unpleasing. The old monk, Brother Robert, was kind to him, bringing him soup, lemony drinks, eggs, and medicine, absenting himself so much from his devotions that Owain the Abbot looked in on Howell.

"You're making poor old Robert work pretty hard, aren't you?" he said. "He isn't a nurse, you know. You don't look too bad to me. Why don't you get out of there and do something quiet, not too taxing? I've excused you

118

your Offices until you're quite well. I've got some rather nice pages of illuminated manuscript just come in— make a penny or two for us. Come on, lad. brace up. Remember what Saint Paul tells us—"

"I want my mother," said Howell.

Chapter 8

The stars were out now. By leaning far out of the galley window, it was possible to see one or two, very far away and dim, because of the lights on earth: of the night sky, one could get no picture. Exactly what Romeo was thinking of when he remarked that the brightness of Juliet's cheek would shame the stars, as daylight doth a lamp. Or was he? Lazy and well fed, kneeling up at the window, Doran couldn't be bothered to think it out.

Bill was by the fire she had made in the living room, Grip asleep in his corner with his head under his wing. One of the ancient books was on Bill's knee—she must get a look at it when she had the chance. But as well as these peaceful companions, who let her search for stars and think random thoughts, she admitted a shadowy third. Someone to clarify her mind.

Dr. Thorndyke was well used to his surroundings, unconcerned that the district was somewhat brighter and cleaner than when the Ratcliff Highway snaked its sinister way past filthy lodging houses where sailors were robbed and murdered, and an anarchist agent carried Death around with him on a barrow in the form of an infected flea circus.

He was there now, his noble profile against the dark sky, the smoke from his expensive cigar twining round them, a cloud of it sometimes blowing into the room on a night breeze.

She wished she could smell its fragrance. A real cigar would smell luscious. But this one was only fueled by fancy, the cigar tip glowing in her mind's eye . . .

"This is an odd and unusual evening for you, dear young lady," he observed.

"Very. I was just wondering why I'm still here."

"Perhaps," he suggested delicately, "because of the absence of the other member of the household, the secretive and dubious Miss Haddock."

"True. I wouldn't be here if she was. But she won't be back tonight; I feel sure of that."

"The nightlife of Brighton offering more attractions? You may well be right. Does she not strike you as extraordinarily callous for one of your merciful sex, and in this day and age?"

"In any day and age I should think she'd be classified as an absolute stinker, a Beast of Belsen. Leaving that poor man without food or comfort, helpless as he is."

"Do we know the cause of his disability? As a medical man I should be most interested to be told. Obviously not multiple sclerosis, or, I should judge, poliomyelitis."

"Well, I haven't asked. One doesn't."

"Of course not. But that seems to me only one of the mysteries abounding in this family—if 'family' is the appropriate word. Why is Miss Poll so unfeeling towards her uncle? Why does he accept her treatment with such resignation, instead of calling upon outside help, as is his right? Why was that rather large and conspicuous bird not visible when you paid your first visit?"

"Oh. I hadn't thought. It should have been, shouldn't it. Bill said a warder from the Tower had brought it."

"In Miss Poll's absence, I would suggest. Does she

121

seem to you a female who would be fond of domestic pets?"

"Far, far from it."

"So the uncle is prepared to go against her in some matters. Now: you are an expert in the world of antiquities."

"Oh, I wouldn't say that."

"Too modest by half. I must say I know a little of it myself."

"Yes—the house in Queen Square, and the maddening Mr. Penrose and his fabulous hoard, and the curiosity shop in Soho—you know a lot, not a little."

Thorndyke purred. "Gems, coins, ancient manuscripts . . . all pleasant objects in themselves, and a refreshing change from the minutiae of crime—not to mention that the study of them provides an agreeable byway to the past, away from the bustle and noise of the present."

Which present did he mean, Doran wondered—1911? But he was meditating aloud again.

"For instance, the carvings in the living room, which you studied with interest—of what did they remind you?"

"Oh. I'd forgotten them. I don't know. The Bayeux Tapestry—the British Museum—and I believe heraldic devices crossed my mind—but all a bit far back for me. My field is more Stuart and Georgian. But there was something . . . I can't quite bring it to mind. What did they remind *you* of?"

But she realized that what was in his mind would first have to be in hers.

He smiled. "Shall we say, 'old, unhappy, far-off things, and battles long ago'? Or even, 'sad stories of the deaths of kings, how some have been depos'd, some slain in war—' "

" 'Some haunted by the ghosts they have depos'd,' "
Doran finished. "Yes, that's getting nearer. Dr. Thorndyke, do you think there's anything supernormal about
all this?"

"My dear Miss Fairweather (I know you prefer to be
addressed by your professional name), I have investi-
gated several cases of alleged supernatural manifestations. One turned out to be an ingenious trick with
mirrors, another something very similar, involving a sinister Chinaman who was nothing of the kind. But I have
never, alas, encountered any traveler returned from that
bourn they are not supposed to leave, once they have
reached it."

"No? Pity."

"I think you will find at the heart of this mystery an
older mystery still, in a place of blood and darkness.
Which reminds me that time is getting on, and Polton
will be anxiously awaiting me with, no doubt, one of his
excellent little dinners. Yes, it's high time I returned to
my own pleasant bourn at King's Bench Walk . . ."

He had gone, as swiftly evanescent as the cloud that a
moment ago hid the young moon. Doran sighed. All very
well to play literary detective games with oneself. One
might as well summon up Holmes and get him to have
Poll committed to the Female Penitentiary, for which she
seemed to be admirably fitted. Except that in Holmes's
day it would have been the rope, for the murder of Malcolm Grover.

And none of these clever bachelors could have sorted
out poor Bill and his problems, as she had done that day.
Doran doubted if even Lady Molly of Scotland Yard or
Loveday Brooke, Lady Detective, could have cooked a
perfect steak in Stone Age conditions . . .

She went back to Bill, and was rewarded by his rare

smile, which seemed to have wonder in it as well as gladness to see her. As he put down the book he had been reading she used her gift for reading things upside down to make out its title, which was *The Great Chronicle of London.* Its binding looked newer than some of the other volumes.

"I don't know what I'm still doing here," she said. "If you're exhausted, throw me out."

"Not bloody likely. Sorry."

"That's all right. I've heard the phrase before. And it *was* used by a rather famous young woman, of course."

He looked puzzled. Conversation with him was full of moments when he seemed to have no idea what she was talking about, whilst at others he came back with the right answer immediately. She put it down to Poll's very limited vocabulary, the lack of media communications (no television, no radio, few newspapers beyond the tabloids, judging by the evidence), and sheer lack of human company. Perhaps the Tower warder was a good talker. She hoped so. What an Eliza Doolittle this pupil would make: a whole education to supply.

She proposed a nightcap. "Mulled wine. Good traditional stuff. Some of the Sauvignon I brought wouldn't be insulted. Got any spice? Don't answer that; I'm sure you haven't. Well, never mind, we'll just have it warmer than it should be."

The wine, warmed in the hearth, was pleasant enough. Bill seemed relaxed, calm: perhaps she would get answers to questions.

"Where did you go to school?"

"The local comprehensive."

"And was it good? Did you like it?"

"All right, I suppose."

"What did you plan to do with your life?"

124

Bill shrugged. "Didn't have much chance. Me and me sister, we had Dad to look after."

"Why couldn't your mother look after him, if he needed it?"

"She'd gone. And he was a very old man."

Doran remembered. The father had married twice, after a long interval, and the brother and sister replaced the dead children from the first marriage, but he had never cared much for them. It was an ugly domestic picture, which Doran would rather not have looked into closely, but the truth was in there somewhere.

"I'd have gone to sea, given the chance," Bill volunteered. "Then Liz got married, and I didn't have the choice, as there was a kid on the way. Polly."

"But you did work."

"Yeah. I got jobs on the boats, and I got it all mapped out to train for the PLA."

"The—?"

"Port of London Authority. But he—Dad—wanted me home. I thought Liz might come back when her chap hooked it, because Dad made a pet of the baby, always wanted her around."

"And?" This was being a very slow, reluctant story.

"Well, Liz went off, in the end, with her husband. Don't know where. She used to talk about the States. But she left Poll behind."

"What? For you to look after?"

"Yeah."

"Presumably your father helped."

"Couldn't, much. He was over eighty then."

And she treats you like this, when you were father and mother to her, Doran thought indignantly. But the important thing was to get the facts.

"How old was she when her mother left?"

125

"Seven. Dad taught a lot, though, like reading and history."

"*History?* Why that, in particular?"

Bill frowned. "What is this, a quiz, or some sort of job interview?"

"No, it isn't. But I feel there's something odd—something wrong—about your life here, and I want to put it right if I can—that's why I'm asking all these questions."

His eyes met hers, and they were defensive. "Seems to me when you was a parson's wife you got the habit of asking questions and putting your oar in people's lives. Well, that might do in a little country village, but it don't here. See?"

Doran was silent. Then she said, "I deserved that. Sorry. I'm an inquisitive, meddling bore, I know!"

"No—my fault. I shouldn't 'a said that; I spoke out of turn."

"No, you'd every right, and I'll shut up if you want me to. Only—Bill, I *know* there's something behind all this, Poll's rotten behavior, and the way you live. Why did you say people keep away because they're frightened of the stories—what stories? There's a secret somewhere in your past, isn't there?"

After a long pause, he said, "Yes."

"You can tell me about it. I'm not a Social Services secret agent. I won't tell anybody. Please."

"I can't," he said. "I'd like to, it'd be a relief, but I can't. Not my secret to tell. I swore an oath I can't break. Understand?"

"No, I don't understand. People don't usually swear oaths nowadays—and then only in courts of law, where they can mean anything—or nothing."

"This oath wasn't sworn nowadays. It goes back long before me—or you, or any of us."

126

"That doesn't make it any more binding. Less so, probably. Is it a sort of family oath?"

He nodded.

"Anything to do with religion? You're a Catholic, aren't you?"

"Yes."

"And does your confessor approve of it?"

Bill looked away from her. "He doesn't even know about it. I don't go to Mass; I don't take the Sacrament. I'm a lost soul in the Church's eyes. What does it matter what becomes of me?"

"What absolute garbage!" Doran flared. "My husband took a Service of Commination once. Do you know what that is? No, I thought not. It's a curse pronounced from the pulpit on all the people doomed to go down into the fire everlasting. 'Cursed is he that smiteth his neighbor secretly. Cursed are the unmerciful. It is a terrible thing to fall into the hands of the living God: He shall pour rain down upon the sinners, snares, fire and brimstone, storm and tempest—' "

"Stop it! Stop it!" His hands were over his ears.

"I'm only telling you that you're not a sinner—you couldn't be, you poor innocent. If anything, I'd say you were a martyr. Oh, Bill, don't." He was sobbing now, dry sobs that shook his big frame. She stroked and patted him as if he were a heartbroken child, dropped kisses on his hair, wrapped her arms tightly round his shoulders and held him until the weeping subsided. Storm and tempest . . .

Fool, she told herself, stupid mindless idiot, interfering with what doesn't concern you and bringing all this on. Now see what you've done. How are you going to make up for it?

127

On the river a boatful of people passed, roaring unmusically. It was to be hoped the person steering it had stuck to mineral water. Doran thought of Mr. Bob Sawyer and other young gentlemen who smoke in the streets by day and shout and scream in the same by night. There were a lot of them about still, more than Dickens could have imagined.

The noise died away and the night was quiet. Then a clock somewhere not far away struck twelve; from the tower of some still serviceable Hawksmoor church, perhaps. Serviceable in every sense. Felicitous phrase. The fire had gone out.

Bill gently extricated himself from her arms, fumbled for a handkerchief, and mopped his face.

"Sorry," he said. "What a carry-on. Not used to good food or drink, that's it."

"Is it? I should have said you were tired and emotional—not in the usual sense. I promise not to badger you with any more questions. Come on, time you were in bed."

"Yes."

She turned the key in the lock of the main door, drew the bolt she was pleased to find at the top, in case Poll should decide on a late-night return. Bill watched her.

"You're staying here?"

"What else? I'm not about to try my luck on foot round here."

"But you haven't got any night things with you."

"Polly has plenty up in her room. Have you seen it, by the way? No, I thought not. Well, it's very comfortable, for those who like—" *nauseating kitsch*, she had been going to say, but it wasn't fair to use words like that to Bill. She substituted, "It's very comfortable, when one

128

gets used to Polly's style of furnishing. Now, can you get yourself to bed?"

"I do it every night. If you could bring Grim—Grip in, so he won't get lonely."

"If he'll let me—I'm not a very experienced bird handler." But the raven was sleepy and well fed. When picked up, still wrapped in his blanket, he opened one eye and shut it again, gave a faint squawk, and subsided. Doran carried him into Bill's Spartan cell and put him down as near the window as possible. Bill wheeled himself into the room, next to the bed, and handed Doran a candlestick that stood with several others on a little table.

"You'll need this, and matches. And the sitting room lamp'll need putting out." Doran did this, silently cursing those who had left this place without electricity. Then, at Bill's door, she lit her candle and looked back at him.

He was watching her with the look she imagined ghosts must wear, when they revisit the world of the living and know, bitterly, that they *are* ghosts, who can never pass beyond the veil of ectoplasm that makes up a faint likeness of what they once were: never touch, taste, or feel again.

"Goodnight," she said, and lit her way up the dark, dangerous stairs.

Bill lay unsleeping in the silent room, wishing he were dead. His feelings were very much those of Doran's imagined ghost. He had seen and touched Heaven; now he was back in the cold and joyless hell to which the Oath had condemned him. The raven stirred uneasily, as if sensing its master's unrest. Across the river, the clock that had struck midnight chimed the half hour.

Almost before the bell note died away, the door opened softly. A light shone in Bill's eyes, startling him

129

into full consciousness. Poll, furtively returned, with murder in her mind?

But a vision was in his cell, the sort that chastity-famished monks dreamed of, a radiantly beautiful woman, naked as Eve, holding a candle whose gold light showed him all of her. She leaned over him: from her breasts came a faint sweet perfume.

"Are you awake?" Doran asked. "I thought you must be." She slipped into the narrow bed beside him, blew out the candle, and was in his arms, the whole lovely length of her, stopping his words with her kisses, her hands caressing his body, so hurt in the past, now suddenly whole and strong for her.

How fortunate that she had put the *Jeunesse Dorée* in her purse, Doran thought, before she ceased to think and gave herself over to joyful unrestrained passion.

Rodney was not sure where he was when he woke. The merciful uncertainty lasted for all of a minute; then the dreadful scenario was upon him again, and the unpleasant feeling that does indeed resemble a sinking of the heart, if such a thing were anatomically possible.

It was hideously early, but the unmistakable atmosphere of Sunday morning made that no hardship. He showered and dressed, carelessly, not noticing that his right sock failed to match his left, or that his tie was a gloomy grey-green one, the color of pond water. Doran had pronounced it fit only to be thrown out.

The hotel was geared to early risers, with so many tourists to provide for. A waitress smiled at him bravely, showed him to a table (he could have taken any one in the huge dining room), and provided him with what she called a Continental breakfast, a repast of quite good coffee, cold fruit juice, toast and marmalade, as tasteless to him as a helping of cattle fodder would have been, he thought. "Good hay, sweet hay hath no fellow," he said aloud.

The waitress had heard it all before and never attempted riposte or comment. She smiled and passed on.

Rodney's stroll by the river and through deserted streets brought him at last to a church whose notice board advertised Holy Communion at 8:00 A.M. every Sunday. It was locked. Rodney sighed. For years he had fought to keep St. Crispin's open day and night, but the forces of common sense and reality had now decided otherwise. This newish church didn't look as though it would contain anything comparable to his own parish treasures, but he understood: they didn't want their hassocks and altar cloth nicking, either.

He sat down on a low wall and waited, trying to concentrate on images of church vandalism, from the terrible time of Cromwell, when a person known as (he thought) Blue Dick had gone round Canterbury Cathedral with a ladder, gleefully smashing priceless windows and sacred images, paying particular attention to the glorious Christchurch Gate.

At last one or two parishioners arrived, a handful of old women and a youth. Normally Rodney would have chatted to them, but he could think of nothing to say. The priest arrived, a healthy-looking young man very casually robed. Evidently he lived nearby and preferred to don his cassock at home. Rodney hoped he had a good wife.

He reflected afterwards, to his shame, that he had taken in nothing of the church interior, he whose hobby such places were, except for a dim impression that there was a lot of exposed brick and plain window glass.

Even more to his shame—horror, even—he could give nothing at all to the service. It was in Tudor English, not

131

the banal Alternative Service he despised. But the ancient phrases that he had repeated so many hundreds of times went by him as meaninglessly as conversation heard far off and not comprehended. He rose from his knees, went back to a pew, and tried to pray.

It was impossible, for the first time in his life.

The brief service was over, the blessing pronounced. At the south door the little congregation was shaking hands with its vicar, the old ladies (Eleanor Rigbys to a woman) holding on to his strong young fingers, chatting compulsively, as the lonely will, careless that he very much wanted to get home to breakfast before morning service proper. Rodney hesitated when it came to his turn, looked into the eyes of the young man who greeted him cheerfully as a welcome stranger and saw a question there, then passed on, the question unanswered.

He wished he were a Roman Catholic and could have made confession to a priest. Forgive me, Father, for I have sinned. Mea culpa, mea maxima culpa. I have shut myself off from the company of my wife and driven her off, O wretched and miserable sinner that I am.

He even toyed with the idea of doing this—Charlotte Brontë had done it in Brussels, and a more stubborn little Protestant-reared person, it would be hard to find. But he was in a place stranger to him than Brussels, and even if he found a Catholic church, it would now be caught up in hourly masses.

And so he walked, an endless circumlocutory walk that took him to strange tall buildings, some that had once been warehouses and were now offices, dwellings, and restaurants, all with that strange Sunday pall on them that has nothing to do with the ringing of church bells or the absence of people from the streets. He found Island Gardens, paused to look at the very blossom tree that

132

Doran had noticed, strolled down the steep slope at the end of which lay Brunel's invisible tunnel, below the river, and beyond it the improbable fairyland beauty of Greenwich.

He had dined there once with Doran, at the Trafalgar, where they had eaten whitebait (though Doran hadn't liked all the eyes looking up reproachfully at one) and talked of Dickens and Bella Wilfer, and all the fishes that swim in the sea, and Disraeli's dining at the vanished Ship over by the *Cutty Sark*. Then they had gone to see the *Cutty Sark* herself and all her lovely shining figureheads.

And suddenly even the memory was unreal because he was standing at the spot to which they had been looking, over the river. For the first time in his life Rodney wondered what it would be like to drown, whether it was such pain as Clarence had experienced in his nightmare.

Thus he achieved two memorable firsts in the course of one Sunday morning.

After futile, tiring hours of walking, he caught a bus to the West End. At least he could visit the streets Doran had known best. Could the "feller" she had gone off with have been a dealer, an old friend? Was it as innocent as that?

But all the shops and galleries were closed, some permanently, with depressing shuttered fronts. There was a little club she had sometimes used in Bruton Street—that was a possibility. He found the place with much difficulty, but the club had gone, replaced by a dress shop.

Utterly dispirited, exhausted, knowing himself to be on a fruitless quest, Rodney went back all the weary way to Copenhagen Court.

Again he tried the apartment. Nobody answered his ring; no voice spoke from the intercom. There was no point where he could sit and watch the entrance—why were there no longer public benches where people could rest after tramping London streets?

Somebody touched him on the arm. It was one of those members of society whom the authorities wish to discourage from sitting, lounging, or sleeping on public benches. His age was indeterminable, but his inattention to daily shaving revealed that he had a white beard.

"Got any change, guv'nor?"

Rodney, startled, felt in his pockets. "Enough for a bus fare?—telephone?" he inquired. It was the only reason he could think of for anybody asking a stranger for change. In central London he had vaguely noticed people sitting or hanging around in the doorways of shops, or lying on steps to public monuments. Many of them had dogs with them. If he had given any thought to the reason for this, he would have concluded that they were waiting for something—to be summoned to a demonstration, perhaps in aid of canine defense. But he gave it no thought.

The seeker after change looked baffled. "Cup o' tea," he suggested. From his complexion and breath, Rodney would have imagined some other beverage might be his preference. He produced a fifty-pence piece and handed it over.

"Ta, guv," said the seeker. Feeling he had got lucky in an unlikely place, from an unlikely punter, he volunteered cheerfully, "We 'ad a murder rahnd 'ere last week."

Rodney jumped with shock. "A murder? Who?"

"Dunno. They keeps things quiet in these sort o' 'igh-rises. Don't tell you nothin.' "

He shuffled away towards the source of his cup of tea, which was on a nearby corner and advertised a karaoke night, go-go attractions, and a Friday quiz.

To Rodney the news was the last straw. If this was a murder scene, Doran was sure to be mixed up in it: possibly the maid as well. Unimaginable horrors began to unfold in his mind, like a dreadful map of an uncharted place. Perhaps the girl's story had been lies. Perhaps Doran had been the murder victim. Perhaps . . . He hurried into the street as well as he could on his aching, burning feet, and by the day's first piece of luck, arrived at the minicab depot that Gwenllian had used. One of its polite, respectable drivers took him to his hotel.

Some ten minutes after he had left, Doran returned to Copenhagen Court.

She was in a cheerful, uplifted mood. It had been a good day. When she had appeared downstairs, Bill's room had been empty. He was already dressed and in his chair, all the galley windows open, the room bright as she had never seen it. Bill himself seemed to have shed a dimension, as though a porcelain figure had been dusted after long years. He looked young, alert and alive, greeting her with a radiant smile. She debated whether to kiss him, then decided against it.

"Hi," she said. "Morning. I've just looked at my diary and it's Shakespeare's birthday."

"Nice day for it. Hope he's enjoying himself."

"Sure he is. After three hundred and sixty-nine years, he ought to get loads of presents. Tea or coffee?"

"Tea, please. I didn't know whether you was coming down or not."

"Why? Did you think I'd flown away through the roof?"

"Well. I thought you was a sort of dream. Best I'd ever had."

"Well, I wasn't a dream. Here I am, perfectly solid."

135

She knew he was overcome with shyness, and made it easy for him. "Two eggs? Mushrooms? Tomatoes? Sorry, no fried bread, it can't be done. How's Grip?"

"Prime. He finished the meat." The raven was preening his feathers, which now had an iridescent sheen.

"Good. I'll get him some more."

During breakfast Bill said, "I feel I could walk this morning. Unbelievable, ain't it."

"Not at all. It's mostly in the mind."

"Yeah. And if I *could* walk, I'd go to Mass."

Startled and delighted, Doran said, "I'll take you if you like. Think you could manage in a taxi?"

He shook his head. "It might go wrong somehow, and I don't want anything to go wrong this morning."

After breakfast, while Bill enjoyed his usual session by the galley window, Doran gave the room as thorough a cleaning as she could with the scanty materials available. Poll was lucky not to have worse lodgers than those that lurked in corners and cracks: spiders, mostly dead, some unidentifiable creatures resembling the pictures that make the *Encyclopedia Britannica* hazardous light reading, a long-dead mouse, some comatose flies. Resolutely she removed them without killing anything.

In the course of dusting she got a closer look in morning light at the carvings. Without doubt they were very ancient and the work of a skilled craftsman. There was a majesty about them, as though someone in the house had lived and moved in Court circles centuries ago. No Tudor roses—now, that was odd—no Tudor initials, HR or ER. The dragon wasn't a particularly Welsh dragon. The person on the throne was definitely a king, holding orb and scepter.

A wipe of her damp cloth revealed writing: very faint, its black paled to grey, the first word tailing off where

136

plaster had crumbled. But it was readable. It began
LO . . .

LO what? Love? Look? Nothing, Latin or English,
came to mind. Perhaps it was Norman-French. If she
plied Bill tactfully, vulnerable as he must be this
morning, he might tell her what was the secret and the
curse of this house.

It was strange and wonderful to be busy with these
tasks and yet be able to glance up and see the man who
had been her lover last night. Self-deception was not one
of Doran's faults. From her first meeting with Bill she
had known that she wanted him, that his looks roused her
still extremely healthy hormones. She had been cheated
of Henry, and there had been others for whom she had
not been prepared to break her marriage vows.

But Rodney had neglected her for months now. Possibly he had lost all desire for her—husbands did, one
heard, when habit and familiarity killed a wife's attractions. If one were to justify adultery, he had committed it
first with Tiggy—now again, possibly, since Tiggy's
unaccountable return into their lives. But Doran was not
inclined to self-justification this morning.

Last night had not been a landmark in the world's history of seductions. Bill's strange disability and long
years of continence had not equipped him as a Giovanni.
But then she, not he, had been the seducer, and because
she had fallen in love with him, mind and body, she took
her pleasure of him as freely as would a man of the
woman he had pursued and won. There was a triumphant
charm in the situation: she was Semele, conquering a
moon-dazed Endymion, Venus, winning a bewildered
captive Mars. She gave and received delight in full mea-
sure. At last her cheated body was appeased and satisfied.
She was free and happy, at last.

137

They had spoken little. He had accepted her with a wonderful readiness—no apologies, no excuses, only a joyfully returning skill. Just once she had said, "Can't I call you Will—William? I really hate Bill, and it doesn't suit you."

"I *am* Will. But I can't call myself that, ever."

"Why?"

"It was a promise."

"Part of the Oath?"

"Yes."

With that she had to be content. But slyly, the next morning she said, "More tea, Will?" and he had answered yes before he could stop himself. He gave her a long, considering look.

"Women. They get you. Well, all right. But just us."

"Just us."

"Be careful."

"Why?"

"I can't tell you now. It'd be dangerous for you. Now, that's enough. These eggs are great."

"Best free range. I never buy anything else."

She noticed, with fond amusement, that his accent was improving slightly. He must have a quick ear which picked up her own intonations as they talked. She enjoyed the original one, but it was good to know that he was clever enough to transform himself.

Later that morning she went shopping, back to the little supermarket, and laid in more frozen supplies, milk, and bread. As soon as the pub she had been to before opened, she asked the landlord to refreeze the units in her cold box. While this was being done she sat outside and slowly, happily drank a lager.

After they had eaten their midday meal she said, "Will. I have something to tell you."

138

"You're going."

"I must. I've got to go home. They don't know where I am and they'll be going frantic. I'm getting a bit frantic myself, actually, about leaving the children so long, and Vi's not going to forgive me if I stay away longer—quite right, too. And I've got to ring the police about old Mal Grover. They didn't go so far as to accuse me of murdering him, or ask me not to leave town, but I feel I ought to contact them."

Will sighed. "Maybe you ought. When will you go— to Kent, I mean?"

"Tomorrow, early. That'll mean I'll be going the other way from the rush-hour commuter traffic. I'll ring home and explain tonight."

"Well, I'll try and put up with it, but it'll be like . . . I dunno. The sun going out. You're my sun, Doran. And moon as well. I thought last night you was a vision."

Doran began one of her blushes, putting her hands to her cheeks.

"Oh dear. Sorry, I still do this, at my age, too. I'm slightly surprised I still *can* blush, after the way I've behaved. Don't worry, they pass off gradually."

"Speaking of . . . behavior," Will said, "can I make a suggestion?"

"Of course."

"Let's go to bed."

After she had gone, Will lay drowsily meditating on the miracle that had happened to him. He still found it hard to believe that his life could have changed so suddenly and wonderfully. Yet there was the impression of his love's head on the pillow, the warmth of her body still within the sheets, her perfume in the air. It was gloriously true. There was a God: sometimes he had doubted.

139

The sound of the street door opening quickened his heart. She had come back for something; she was here. He sat up, his eyes on the door.

It opened, and Poll came in.

Chapter 9

His first thought and fear was that she would at once detect Doran's recent presence. He must protect her, as well as he could.

" 'Ello," Poll said. "You took bad? No, I can see yer not. Look better'n when I see yer last."

"No thanks to you," Bill said. "You left me all weekend with nothing fit to eat."

She shrugged. "Don't want much usually, do yer. So what's the game—restin'? Sunday afternoon kip?" A sound from Grip attracted her attention. "That thing still alive? Thought it'd 'ave 'opped the twig by now."

"You didn't leave anything for him, either—stale rolls and leftovers."

"Yeah." Poll smiled. "And they eats better'n that in the Tower. Meat, an' little birds, an' mice . . . I could fetch some mice up from the cellar an' you could watch it eat them. Like that?"

"No, I wouldn't. He's all right; he's been fed."

"Oh?" Her face darkened with suspicion. "Who by? And you bin fed, too, I can see that. What's bin goin' on? That Tower guy called again? Because I'm not 'avin' it, see. I'll warn 'im off, he'll get the bum's rush from me if 'e pokes his nose in 'ere again."

"He's not been," Bill said wearily. She would find out

about Doran; there was nothing he could do. She rushed out to the galley, where he could hear her exclaiming and swearing as she made discoveries. Then her footsteps clattered upstairs. A few moments and she was back, her face scarlet with temper.

"*She's* bin 'ere—that tart—'asn't she! Nice taste she's got, French cheese and froze fancy stuff, and all that fruit—and wine, too. God, you've bin goin' it, you two. Feed you up like a fightin' cock, did she? Not a lot in it for 'er, though, was there—no fight and no cock. Christian charity, was it—poor old man needin' care and attention? She'll get some time off in purgatory for that, she will—"

"They don't have indulgences in her church, Poll. And it wasn't charity; it was kindness."

"Oh yeah? She can keep 'er bloody kindness. *And* she's a thief. Taken a silver photo frame off my dressing table, an' a brooch an' a teddy—that's what you'd call cami-knickers when you was a boy, only you wouldn't know abaht women's stuff now, would yer, poor old sod. I'll get 'er for those, I will."

Bill knew quite well that these things were Doran's, stolen from her by Poll: she had merely taken back her own. He guessed that the frame had held a picture of one of her children, and that the garment was new, never worn. Doran would not have taken anything that had touched Poll's body.

"They were here," he said. "I expect she didn't want them to go to Brighton." Without ever having seen Poll's room, he guessed that it was full of pretty things she had stolen and kept for herself. For one thing, he was glad— Poll had not accused Doran of using her room, or picked up the traces of her perfume, either there or down here. For that he had to thank Poll's own scent, powerful and

142

recently applied. He wondered what man she slept with in Brighton—men, more likely.

Poll sat on the edge of his bed and stared him in the face. " 'Ere, there's summink I gotter know. You 'aven't told her, 'ave you?"

"Told her what?" But he knew.

"The Secret."

"No, of course not. I swore not to. Don't you know me better?"

Still the basilisk stare. Never a beauty, Poll looked at this moment like a gargoyle, a stone woman's head with blank eyes and a thin line for a mouth.

"No, I don't know yer at all. Not now. What's come over yer? Answerin' back, saucin' me, facin' me out. Well, drop it! I'm the Powerful one, remember; you're just the wimp that crops up in the Family now an' then. You been drinkin', I daresay, an' it's made you frisky. Well now, We'll 'ave to do summink abaht that."

She went out and shut the bedroom door. Bill could hear her clattering and banging, swearing as she dropped something, lumbering up the stairs as if burdened. He had a cold fear that he knew what she was doing, after several repetitions of the sounds.

She came back into the room and began a grotesque pursuit of Grip, ignoring Bill's protests. While the bird squawked and struggled, she drove it into a corner and wrapped it in a rug, cursing it all the time. Once it bit her and she screamed and banged it with her fist. She could hardly carry it, dumpy as she was, but in the end she got it through the door and down the stairs. Bill could hear no more. When she came back she was red-faced, breathing hard, triumphant.

"What have you done with him?" Bill demanded. "You've not killed him?"

143

"That great soddin' thing? What with? A poleax? No, I got plans for your little pet. When I go, it goes too. An' if yer wants to know where, into the river. Can't swim, can it, and won't float, I'll see to that."

"I think you're a devil."

She preened. "Yeah, I am, aren't I. Now I'll tell yer the rest of it. All the stuff what *she* brought, that slag, I've took upstairs, except what I've thrown out. So no little snacks on yer own. Oh, and no little rides either."

Under his appalled eyes, she wheeled his chair out of the room, leaving the door open so that he could see her take it to the farthest corner of the galley and tip it over. Even if he reached it, it would be beyond his strength to get it right way up.

"Poll," he said, "don't. What have I done to you? You used to be—kind to me once, in your way. Why are you against me now?"

"Why?" She leaned forward and stabbed at him with her finger. "Because you're a effin' traitor, that's why. You let an outsider in, and if I don't stop it, you'll give me away—me and your dad and all the others, not that they'd find much left to charge 'em with after all this time—though I'll make sure a bit of it 'its the 'eadlines. Won't make page three, though!" She laughed. "Funny color you've gone, *Uncle*. Well, I thought I was 'ome for the night, but seems I'm not. I'll just pack a few bits, then I'm off."

"Where? Where? Poll, for God's sake, don't leave me like this."

She smiled, a sneering gargoyle. "It'll be a pleasure."

He was glad to see, as she shut the door, a bloody streak on her arm and the gash where the raven's beak had torn it.

* * *

144

He was quite alone and helpless. He covered his eyes and prayed, a rosary of Hail Marys and Paternosters, then the names of all the saints he could remember. Then he finally crossed himself and thought of his situation. There was no saying when Poll would be back: the only certainty was that she would stay away long enough to torture and humiliate him.

The prayers had strengthened him. In his mind's eye he could see the bare room filled with faces, kindly, beautiful, benign, willing help towards him because he had somehow kept a gleam of faith alive in the house of the Devil.

That morning, alight with euphoria, he had said to Doran that he almost felt he could walk. But now he knew that had been only hope, with no substance. After so many years of inactivity, his leg muscles were weakened, the flesh fallen away into slackness—it would take months, perhaps a year, of exercise to restore them. He could move his legs enough to get from the bed into his chair, but it was an effort, and painfully slow.

He might manage to roll himself out of the bed onto the floor, and crawl his way about. But what if he was unable to raise himself again, and could only lie prone, worse off than before? Nobody would hear his cries, in this house whose walls were over a foot thick. If he could only get to the window and signal to the river . . .

It was worth trying. Thinking one step at a time, he threw the coverlet onto the floor, so that at least he would fall soft. Then, setting his teeth against the shock, he managed to roll himself to the extreme bed edge, clear of the thin blankets and sheets. It looked an alarming drop to the ground. But with another great effort he made it, and fell.

The shock was violent. He fell on his back and lay

helpless as an upturned beetle. Muttering encouragement to himself, he struggled to raise himself by his elbows, straining his neck and shoulders until he could drag himself towards the wall at the head of the bed. This gave him a support to lean against—if only he could propel his upper half so far.

He would never do it.

But he did. Sweating, pierced with shooting pains, at last he was half sitting against the wall.

"Thank God," he said, over and over again. Then he set himself to the enormous task of crawling and dragging himself across the floor, trusting only in the strength of his arms and shoulders. The sky began to darken as the afternoon shadows fell.

Doran woke early next morning, excitedly conscious that she was going home. No more nights in this suffocating place, no more strange days out of time. It wasn't too early to telephone—someone would be about; Armorel would see to that. Armorel! A shiver of excitement went through her as she dialed the number of Bell House.

Vi answered. A curious-sounding Vi, unlike her calm self.

"Vi? It's me."

There was a distinct pause before Vi said, "Yes, Miss Doran. We were wondering."

"I know I've been an awful time getting in touch, but you see—oh, I can't go into it all now, but I'll tell you when I get home."

"You're coming home, then?"

"Well, of course! What else?" She knew nothing of Poll's lying message, which Vi had heard, of the conclusions that had been reached. She had been casual, preoccupied, had left them without news too long, and they weren't very pleased with her—that was all. "Can I speak to Rodney?" she asked.

"Mr. Rodney's in London," answered the same cold voice, "looking for you. He was very worn-out when he rang last night, and not very well."

"Oh. I don't understand, Vi. Why was he looking for me? What's the matter? Are the children all right?"

"As well as can be expected," said Vi in her iciest tone. She had never before spoken so to Miss Doran, but this time her employer had gone too far.

"I still don't understand, and I've said I'm sorry. Where is Rodney?"

"Towerview. It's a big hotel, he says."

"I'll go there as soon as I've had breakfast. Give my love to Kit and Armorel and say I'll be home soon: we both will. 'Bye."

She hung up before she could hear the disparaging sniff that was Vi's signal of extreme disapproval.

The half hour that followed was a rush of packing and eating a skimped breakfast. Realizing that haste in itself was pointless, Doran put on the kitchen television and watched it idly in an attempt to slow herself down. The early news bulletin was on, the usual catalogue of wars, road protests, and politicians' opinions. Suddenly she put down her second piece of toast as a familiar view appeared on the screen: Tower Bridge, veiled in morning mist.

"A couple walking by the Thames early today in the Tower Bridge area at Wapping," said the newsreader, "were drawn to investigate a spot on the foreshore where excavations seemed to have been taking place. Police called to the site discovered what appeared to be the

147

remains of two children buried under layers of river deposits."

A girl was shown in close-up, very damp-haired and excited, with a silent boyfriend in the background, explaining hurriedly that they had been on the lookout for anything interesting that might have been washed up when they saw this sign stuck on a pole, and the sand roughed about underneath, so as they happened to have a spade with them (mud larks, Doran thought, hunting for Thames treasure), they started digging and uncovered bones. At that moment the newsreader cut her off with the remark that more news of the discovery would be given when the police had anything to report. Cut to next item.

Doran, toast forgotten, abandoned any attempt to eat. She knew exactly the place, among the rows of ancient stairs leading down to the Lower Pool, and she would be on the spot as soon as she could return the keys of 52 Copenhagen Court. After all, it was on her way to Rodney's hotel.

She managed to find a parking spot for her car near Wapping Old Stairs. (Could it have been less than a week since she had driven past the street sign and thought of Molly of the ballad, who protested her constancy to her Jack rather too earnestly to be convincing?)

The presence of a small crowd told her that she had found the right spot. Grisly news travels fast. There was a police cordon round a group of men digging the sand and silt, glimpses of checkered police hatbands, the girl of the television interview easily recognizable, being badgered by members of the public and (Doran guessed) the press.

And, on the edge of the police inside the cordon, the never-to-be-forgotten face of Detective Inspector Moray.

148

Doran made her way forward, trying to look as inconspicuous as possible. Her long legs made swift progress easy: she sneaked up on him before anyone could stop her.

"Detective Inspector Moray? Remember me—Doran Chelmarsh, er, Fairweather. Copenhagen Court. And the mortuary."

His expression said that he remembered her all too well, and wasn't pleased to see her, but he greeted her politely enough.

"Good morning, madam. Can I help you?"

"Well, I wondered if you'd found what you're looking for. I saw the TV news—"

"They all did, madam, and they all want the same as you, but I'm afraid nobody is allowed past this spot. If I could ask you kindly to wait until official reports are published . . ."

"It's only that—I've had a good deal to do with murder investigations—I think I told you, didn't I? Mostly with the Kent police—Detective Inspector Grimwade would remember me . . ."

"Grimwade? Yes, he's at the Yard now." It never did any harm to be in with someone who'd got a spectacular and unlikely promotion, as Moray hoped to do. "Well, just for a moment, mind. There's not a lot to see." Swiftly, unobtrusively, he lifted the rope. Doran ducked under and was standing behind one of the diggers. As he straightened his back she looked down into the hole.

Bones, recognizably. Strangely dark, not the white bones of popular supposition. And very—yes, two of them had been lifted and laid on the surface. Very small indeed. Doran, the vegetarian, had not had much to do with animal bones, but she knew approximately the size of the parts of a leg of lamb, and these were no larger.

149

Moray was telling his workmen to disturb the bones as little as possible. Their pointed spades were poking and prodding among the remains. Doran looked away, momentarily sickened. Nearby lay a large white piece of cardboard or wood with a death's-head and crossbones crudely crayoned or painted on it: the attention catcher.

Quite suddenly Doran's mind cleared of certain fogs that had been obscuring it lately. "The year 1483. The White Boar. 'At last Richard took the scepter.' Miles Forest. John Dighton, Walter Tyrell. Will Slaughter."

Will Slaughter. Bill Slater. "I *am* Will. But I can't call myself that, ever." A descendant of that Black Will whose name had figured among the suspected murderers of the Princes in the Tower, one of Richard III's hirelings.

But that had been five hundred and more years ago. How could the Slaughter family possibly have kept on that house more or less as it had been, all that time, with those obviously Ricardian carvings in the room? What could the family promise have been? Why was Poll such an evil creature? And what was the sense of guilt from which Bill—Will—suffered? Were there other deaths involved, besides those of little Edward V and his brother the Duke of York?

A host of questions propelled Doran to Moray's side again.

"Have you any idea who these children could be?"

A Medusa glare from the spectacled eyes should have turned her to stone on the spot.

"The remains have not yet been examined."

A police doctor was doing just that, in fact, as the bones were lifted carefully by rubber-gloved hands onto a waiting sheet.

"What can he possibly learn from just looking at them like that?" Doran indignantly asked Thorndyke.

"Perhaps ascertaining that the subjects are in fact dead," came the impassive reply. She turned from him as a reporter grabbed her elbow and demanded to know what the police had told her, and whether she herself knew anything. A television cameraman had appeared from somewhere and was angling for a close shot of what was going on. Pointedly asked to move on by another policeman, she did just that, regaining her car to find that it had acquired a ticket, parked as it was in the way of a line of police vehicles.

She remembered the collection of the corpse of "Ophelia" from the river near Abbotsbourne, so long ago, when Rodney had said . . .

Rodney.

Within a few minutes she had reached the hotel, and was parking legally under the direction of a doorman.

"Mr. Chelmarsh? Room 517, madam. Shall I say—"

"No, don't. I'll just go up." The neat receptionist looked apprehensive, as she well might at the spectacle of an untidy young woman with a high color and river mist in her hair rushing off in the direction of a respectable guest's room.

The door of room 517 was opened, after a pause and a distant oath, by Rodney, dressed only as far as his trousers and shirt, half his face covered in shaving cream intermixed with blood from a razor nick.

At the sight of Doran his expression became catatonic with shock and disbelief. He backed away from her as far as the bed, sitting down on it suddenly.

"What . . . what . . ."

She tried to rescue him. "It's really me. Haven't you heard from Vi this morning?"

151

He shook his head.

"Damn, I thought she'd have been on to you as soon as she heard from me."

Slowly he wiped the shaving cream from his face with a towel. "Are you alone?" he asked, bafflingly to her.

"Of course. Gwenllian left days ago. Didn't you know? Do wash your face and stop that cut bleeding. You look as if you'd been in a razor fight."

He turned to the washbasin and sluiced his face, which seemed to restore his power of speech. "I don't understand. She said you'd packed up and gone away—with a man."

"*Who* said? Rodney, there's some awful misunderstanding and we've got to sort it out. Now, get your jacket or something on, ring for some coffee, and let's talk about it." Briskly she took off her coat, straightened her tumbled hair, and settled herself in the armchair, while Rodney stared at her as though he had never seen her before. The coffee arrived almost instantaneously. Doran was glad of hers, and Rodney began to look as though he were emerging from some bad dream.

"Now then," she began. "I'm sorry I didn't get in touch with you at first, but I was pretty angry—about Tiggy turning up like that as soon as I was away. Never mind about that, I'm sure there's an explanation."

"Gwenllian."

"I might have known. Anyway, that was that bit. The next bit was that Gwenllian had a perfectly dreadful old boyfriend, and he disappeared and turned up robbed and murdered, and I had to go and identify him, and would you believe it, the river mortuary is *in* Tower Bridge."

"I'd believe anything."

"You'll need to. Well, Gwenllian had this maid or cleaner or whatever, the most unspeakably brutish girl

you can imagine. She took me to visit—" the story was
getting onto slippery ground; Doran cupped her face in
her hands, praying that her dreaded blush would not
creep up and give her away "—a relation of hers, an
uncle, in the most extraordinary old house you can
imagine, straight out of Harrison Ainsworth. He's a
cripple in a wheelchair and his only friend is a young
raven from the Tower, which was given him by a
yeoman warder. The niece, Polly, who's a thief as well as
a murderer (did I tell you she probably did for Gwenllian's old man?), went off to Brighton to flog her pick-
ings, and left this poor man with nothing to eat and no
means of getting anything, so I did a lot of shopping for
him and the raven— Rodney, what's the matter?"

For Rodney was dissolving into laughter. He lay back
on the bed with shrieks and shouts and peals of mirth that
would have done credit to a canned television audience.
When at last he sat up, moping his streaming eyes, Doran
said mildly, "I'm glad I amuse you."

"My darling, you do more than amuse me—you con-
vince me!" He paused briefly for another outbreak. "Oh
forgive me, I can't stop . . . Such a grotesque, fantastic,
Gothic sequence of events couldn't have happened to
anyone but you, and I believe every word of it—who
could invent it, anyway? So—it must have been the
unspeakably brutish Polly who telephoned me and told
me this nonsense about you having gone off with a man.
Why would she do that?"

"Evil, sheer evil, and a sort of mischief, I suppose."

"That figures. She isn't a hunchback dwarf, by any
chance?"

"No, but there is a hunchback connection—if you
believe the legends, though I think they're Tudor lies.

153

Rodney. if you start again, you'll do yourself an injury—
do sober up and listen."

"I'll try."

Doran told him of the events of that morning, making
it all as factual as she could: she had laid on the fantasy
element deliberately before. Rodney listened, composed
enough now.

"So you think these could be the remains of the
Princes in the Tower?"

"It's possible, yes."

"But they were found—in 1674, wasn't it? Buried
under a staircase in the White Tower. Charles the Second
had them reverently put in a marble urn in Westminster
Abbey, and there they still are."

"But are they? Isn't there a story that a priest buried
them somewhere more holy and dignified than the staircase?" Doran said eagerly.

"I've no idea. If only I had my books here . . .
There've been millions of words written about the whole
thing, whether Richard had them killed because young
Edward was the rightful king, or whether Henry the Seventh was really guilty, and whether the bones were really
them or blood sacrifices of children put there when the
Tower was built. I've read it all, but I can't remember the
arguments."

"Nor can I. In any case, the Thames shore doesn't
seem a particularly holy or dignified place to put them.
And surely somebody would have found them by now."

"One would think so. If a couple of mud larks with a
spade could find them," reasoned Rodney, "they couldn't
have been buried very deep. Of course, Execution Dock
wasn't far away."

"But they wouldn't execute children that size as
pirates."

"What size?"

"Smaller than Kit." Doran shuddered. "What a horrid conversation this is being. I wish I'd never heard that news bulletin."

Rodney regarded her fondly. "If you hadn't, you'd have come rushing up here as soon as it got around. I know you. Let's go home."

"What a good idea." But her agreement dragged a little. Rodney, who did indeed know her, said, "They won't let you in on it, you know. You're not a pathologist; you're not even a professional historian. You could book yourself in at the Savoy for months and they still wouldn't let you near those bones. Mere curiosity won't get you anywhere."

"But I do know the local police. DI Moray, for instance." She described her involvement with the death of Mal Grover and her encounter with Moray at Wapping. "So you see, they know me."

"Well, if you think that being (a) a murder suspect and (b) a member of the snooping public will recommend you to them as a person qualified to have a privileged view of The Bodies and discuss theories, I'm afraid you'll have to think again. Come on—I'm sick of traffic pollution and London streets."

"All right." She heard about the breakdown of Rodney's car and his less-than-enjoyable journey from Barminster. Her car was in the hotel's garage: there was nothing to do but pack Rodney's case, pay his bill, and leave. They should be home for lunch. Doran telephoned Vi, striving to make it all sound normal, but heard a very cool, judgmental voice at the other end.

"It takes a lot to ruffle Vi." she said. hanging up. "but she's seriously ruffled now. I shall have to work hard at being the perfect wife and mother to pacify her. Oh dear."

"I shouldn't worry. With all your faults, she loves you still. So do I."

They kissed, more fondly than for a very long time, Rodney effervescent with relief and Doran deeply thankful that, somehow, things seemed to be all right between them again.

As they drove off, Rodney's eyes were on Tower Bridge, which he sincerely hoped he would never have to see again in his life. The knowledge that it contained a mortuary did nothing to endear it to him.

But Doran, watching the traffic, could still spare a long, thoughtful look at the Tower. Since William the Conqueror's day and before, it had held a million secrets. Now it held another.

They were lucky with the Monday morning traffic. The coast-bound line of it was scanty, the monster transports at a minimum, the public obviously reserving their journeys for Easter. Sooner than could have been hoped, the countryside grew and the streets receded, until the moment—Doran knew exactly when it would come— when the great panorama of Kent lay before them, gentle slopes and meadows, sheep with their lambs, the North Downs brooding protective and welcoming as they had been when London-sick pilgrims joyfully set their sandals on the way to Canterbury. And the road winding towards home.

Rodney looked at his watch. "Good time. I've had an idea."

"Oh, what? It had better be good; I'm carrying an increasing burden of guilt."

"Why not postpone the dreaded hour? Why don't we have lunch out?"

156

"Oh. But the children—"

"Kit's at school. Armorel won't notice if we're out for one more meal. Oh, do say yes. We could go to the Golden Guinea Fowl."

"Mm. Nice food, but I wish the actual guinea fowl weren't so visible." Animal welfare was always in the forefront of Doran's mind.

"That's hypocrisy, if you eat them."

"But I don't—I always have something else, in case you hadn't noticed." This was true: Doran had indulged herself in them once, and indeed they had tasted delicious in their sauce of cream and brandy, but after one had seen the innocent little brown creatures trotting about the garden, it somehow became unimportant how they tasted.

"Right, guinea fowl off the menu. But there are plenty of other things. Felix would be so pleased to see us."

"He'll probably be booked up."

"Not before Easter." Rodney was persistent, for it was very much in his mind that a lot of time had passed since he and Doran had eaten out as a couple in one of their favorite places.

Two telephone calls from a wayside box settled the question. Vi, whom Rodney had nobly undertaken to tackle, graciously agreed that it would be less trouble to do lunch just for Armorel and herself. And Felix exclaimed with delight that he couldn't wait to entertain two of his favorite people, and that he would be at the door with his eyes shaded, scanning the horizon, like the Last Watch of Hero in Thingy's picture.

"I shouldn't have thought he knew who Thingy was," Rodney remarked. "Who was he, anyway?"

"Leighton. And Felix, though you might not think it,

157

was born in Manchester, where they have a horde of gorgeous Pre-Raphaelites."

They were climbing up the Downs, up lanes that looked too narrow for cars, but had strategic lay-bys in the overgrown hedges to avert threatened collisions. The leaves were thickly clustered now, with May in sight, overhanging the lanes like Gothic arches, full of the light, lustrous green of late spring. Lambs bleated and nibbled at the young growth in the hedges, birds sang (one could actually hear them, with no opposition from traffic), and horses looked hopefully from their paddocks. Doran felt she had been exiled from all this for years, and sighed with pleasure when the Golden Guinea Fowl came in sight round a bend.

It was a long, low, white-painted building, three cottages in one, with a wild garden in front and a handsome barn alongside. The doomed (but not by her) guinea fowl were running merrily among daffodils and tulips past their best blooming.

" 'Alas, unconscious of their doom, the little victims play,' " said Rodney.

"Shut up. Oh, look, there he is."

Felix, if not precisely at the door scanning the horizon, can't have been far behind it, for he was welcoming them with embraces almost before Doran had parked. He was a smiling-faced man of indeterminate age and a figure so elegant as to suggest that he went easy on his own brilliant cooking.

"Darlings, so wonderful to see you. Where *have* you been? Now, come through into the arbor and have an ice-cold something—vodka-ton? Martini? Pernod, with ice, of course, or it could mere gin, though I think better of you than that."

With such chatter (by and large sincere, for he entertained a great many stupendously boring and exacting guests) he conducted them to the rustic arbor by the back door of the restaurant, and settled them with drinks on the house. Rodney breathed the unpolluted air with a face of rapture. Doran sipped her drink, unaware that she was pulling a fallen flower to pieces.

Her thoughts wandered, always northwards. What is he doing now? Has Poll given him lunch? What time did she get back yesterday?

Surely she *did* get back, after all, it is her home—isn't it? I wonder if the sandwiches are still fresh.

"Yes," she said to Rodney, "it's getting warmer. This arbor's so sheltered."

Her last sight of Will. His look, as she turned at the door, one of pure love and happiness. Not a shade of reproach for leaving him. She was glad it had been like that.

Would the raven be all right? Poll was certain to make a fuss about it, threaten it, even. But a raven, even a half-grown one, isn't an easy thing to dispose of. And surely—could Poll be all that bad? She'd spoken quite civilly to Will the first time Doran was there. She must have a good side; everyone had.

Will. Not Bill anymore, in her thoughts. How he would love this, the peace, the champagne air, the beautiful fields stretching away to the hills before them, the homely white house. If she'd stayed in Dockland, she would have devised a way of getting him outside. There was a farm there, an urban jewel—he would enjoy that. Perhaps she could arrange it next time: for I *am* good at arranging things, she congratulated herself.

Did Howell's brotherhood or whatever have any sort of retreat, where people could go to recover from stress, and have medical treatment? Howell would enjoy organizing that, and driving Will about. She imagined a charming tiny chapel with a statue of Our Lady—a good, professional one, not the sentimental plaster mock-up too often found in sales among the garden tools and chipped Styrofoam fountains. Will, who said the Latin Grace before Meat, would like that.

They (and by now Doran had herself joined the imaginary party) could drive round Gower, and see the Atlantic breakers roll and roar. They could . . .

"Smoked salmon or fresh peach with garlic cheese?" broke in a voice, seeming to come from miles away. But it was Rodney's, next to her at the rustic table, while Felix stood beside him smiling patiently, notebook at the ready.

"I'm sorry—what did you say?"

"Well, I read out the entire menu for today, but I don't think you heard a word."

"She's driven from London; she's tired," said kind Felix.

"No, no, I'm not tired at all. Smoked salmon, please."

Poll was discovering Kent: not its beauties, but the complexities of getting from one spot to another. Grimly she battled her way through timetables impossible to work out and officials who found her speech difficult to understand and shocking when understood.

"School kids are one thing," said a female bus driver to her companion, "but you'd think they'd have grown out of it at her age. Such nasty words, too."

The nasty words continued under Poll's breath as she tramped down Mays Lane, Abbotsbourne. And the point of her long, exasperating journey.

"Two'd be just right if I'm lucky. But I can make do with one, and she'll mind about the boy most."

160

She found the back garden gate, from which the front door was visible, and crouched among the trees, waiting for Kit.

Chapter 10

Rodney lost no time on their arrival home in going to his books to gather up all the available facts about the mysterious deaths of the little Plantagenet Princes. It was left to Doran to deal with Vi, making her excuses for noncommunication as convincing as possible (though it was sometimes hard to gauge the depth of Vi's conviction). It all went off reasonably well, Doran thought. Her reunion with Armorel was joyful. Several new words had come into Armorel's vocabulary, such as *dem*, meaning her mother's shiny earrings, and *cime*, an attempt at the word *climb*, indicating that she wanted to get onto her mother's knee and demonstrate affection.

Tybalt's reaction to his owner's return was less effusive. As cats will, he registered that he realized she was home, then turned his back on her and pointedly began to wash himself, thoroughly and unnecessarily. Offers of food were met by a cold stare, as of a celebrated cordon bleu expert offered mushy peas out of a tin. He turned from the dish of expensive Luxicat and left, slowly and with dignity.

"Oh well, be like that," Doran told him. She turned with relief, still holding Armorel, to where Rodney sat at the dining table, books all around him, most of them biographies of Richard III.

"It's impossible to get at the truth, because none of them knew it," he said. "Shakespeare was copying More, who was only a child when it all happened. He was a Tudor propagandist out to make Richard into a monster. Listen to what he says, having pinpointed Sir James Tyrell as chief agent. He's writing about a summer night in 1483. I'll summarize. 'Tyrell appointed Miles Forest, a fellow fleshed in murder beforetime, and one John Dighton, his own horsekeeper, a big, broad square knave. When all the other attendants had been sent away, about midnight Forest and Dighton stole upon the innocent children, suddenly lapped them up among the bedclothes, keeping down by force the featherbed and pillows hard unto their mouths, and so dispatched them.' A lot of manpower to deal with two little boys. Then Tyrell had them buried 'at the stair foot, meetly deep in the ground under a great heap of stones.' But Richard, who seems to have been a good Catholic as well as a serial killer, ordered them to be reburied; they were, by a priest, unnamed, who put them somewhere secret and then conveniently died."

"Mm. I did know all that, like everybody else who's read *The Daughter of Time*. Remind me what rewards the murderers got."

"It's hard to trace any. Bits of nonsense information. Miles Forest 'at sainct Martens pecemele rotted away.' "

"Nasty for him. Of what?"

"Doesn't say. John Dighton was presented with the living of Fulbeck, but by Henry the Seventh, not Richard. Another John Dighton was Tyrell's servant, when Tyrell was arrested by Henry on a trumped-up charge. Tyrell got the chop, literally, but Dighton was pardoned, and walks out of history, whistling gaily."

"All very fishy. Anyone else mentioned?"

163

"A John Grene—there seem to have been several. One of them was appointed receiver of the Isle of Wight, and another was pardoned for something unspecified. Oh, and there's Black Will—Will Slaughter."

Doran jumped. "And he was—?"

"In exclusive charge of the Princes, until the night of the murder, according to More, after which he's never mentioned."

Doran sat very still. She had known, but it was odd to hear it confirmed by Rodney.

"For Slaughter read Slater," she said. "He was taken off the job, for which he'd probably been promised a fat reward. He saw the men who did it get pardoned or rewarded, or just fade out. He faded out himself, from the scene, that is, and made his mind up to live for revenge."

"How do you know?"

"I don't; I'm just guessing. I think Will Slaughter collected any perks he could lay his hands on, left the Tower, and set up in a good substantial house far enough away not to be conspicuous. Nobody need know who he was—no media reports in those days—and gradually the name changed. He had a large family and bred them all up to take revenge for the reward he'd been cheated out of."

Rodney stared. "What an unpleasant theory. Revenge on King Richard?"

"No, he died at Bosworth two years later. Revenge on Society, perhaps. A sort of Fagin, only much more evil— I've always liked Fagin. I think Slaughter murdered and robbed, very cleverly, and never got found out—or made himself so feared that nobody dared tell."

"That sort of thing doesn't happen in England."

"No? Henry the Eighth turned into a sort of man-monster."

164

"Yes, but he had limitless power and money and authority."

"Couldn't it have worked on a smaller scale? The medievals weren't like us, were they. Think of the Paston Letters, and how shockingly people behaved—the raids on property, for instance—and *they* were only Norfolk middle-class, or what passed for it. They were crueler, they didn't share our sort of conscience or our rules. Even in the middle of the eighteenth century the law hanged two little girls of eight and eleven *pour encourager les autres*. But why am I telling you this? You know it all."

Rodney pondered, frowning. "Perhaps. I'm prepared to believe in a medieval Bluebeard on the banks of the Thames. But for five hundred years—half a millennium?"

"They were also infinitely more superstitious, God-and-Devil-orientated. I think that house got a name for evil, and as nobody dared burn it down—and it was built of stone, anyway—it went on standing, with the same brainwashed family in it."

"And you're telling me that all the generations between then and now were tainted with this—thing?"

"Not all of them. No. I think that perhaps one dominant person in each generation was brainwashed—perhaps there was a ritual, a sort of initiation ceremony they had to go through, swearing to keep the family oath. But there were divergents, those who couldn't go along with it. They probably said they had a vocation and escaped into convents or monasteries, or simply ran away. Otherwise they'd get punished or rubbed out by Father or Grandmama or whoever."

"I still don't know how you know this. I never remember you having a bent for fiction before."

"I've been to the house, for one thing. I've met two members of the clan, for another. That girl, Poll, is a perfect example of the original Slaughter type. I called her brutish, didn't I, and it was the right word."

Rodney recalled the voice on the telephone, giving him that insidious, lying message. "Yes. I believe you. And what was the old man, the uncle, like?"

Doran's voice was quite steady, and her betraying blush brought no warning heat to her breast and throat. Good. "Actually, he wasn't old. Difficult to tell his age, really, with prematurely white hair. But he was one of the untainted Slaughters—one of the sort who'd have turned to religion."

"Did he get disabled in the war?"

"No, he wouldn't have been old enough." A sudden, blinding revelation had come to her, which she was almost afraid to put into words. "I know how he was injured. He didn't tell me, but I know. His father crippled him."

"What?"

"His father was one of the other sort. Polly was his acolyte; he brought her up and taught her. Will said she was always very interested in history, and I thought that was odd, but I see it now, of course she would be. Will's father was her grandfather. Her mother belonged to his second lot of children, who replaced the ones who died. Who were 'lost,' Will said . . ."

"What's the matter, darling? You've gone pale. What is it?"

"I think—I've just realized what 'lost' means. He killed them—his own children. He had to find blood sacrifices, and they happened to be on hand. I think. I hope to God I'm wrong."

She put her hand on Armorel, who had fallen asleep and lay on the sofa beside her, rosy as a Boucher cherub. "About time we had a cup of tea. Kit will be home any minute." Rodney was profoundly disturbed: he had always recognized true evil when he encountered it.

Kit had spent a pleasant enough day at school. True, it began with maths, not his favorite subject, but it involved the use of computers, which he enjoyed. The school was a civilized one with a high intake of boys who enjoyed learning, some even with careers mapped out. One boy in Kit's class had seriously decided to be an actor; another saw himself as the first Englishman under twenty to walk on the moon. Kit felt he himself might have something to do with music, because he knew that he was rather good at it. He loved books, but had seen that too many of them had turned his father into someone a bit drier and dustier than he need have been. It was bad enough having to wear glasses without becoming the sort of boy who was always poring over books. Bad for one's body, too, and Kit cared very much for cricket, which he had played, after a fashion, since the age of about two.

One bright thought was with Kit all day: when he got home his mother would be there. With luck—you never quite knew with her, and this last week her absence had made Daddy very unhappy. She hadn't even rung him, Kit, which had hurt him a little, even with Tiggy for company.

But he didn't blame her. She was a special sort of lady whom he wouldn't have swapped for any other kind— adventurous as a boy and very skilled at getting him to do things by subtle flattery instead of shouting and nagging.

His friend Hugh usually went part of the way home

with him, but not today—Hugh had to go into Barminster on the bus to see a rotten dentist. So he set off alone, down the drive that led from the school, two large Victorian houses knocked into one, with a modern annex.

Home was nearly a mile and a half's journey on foot, and he'd have to hoof it today because his bike had something wrong with it and Daddy said it wasn't safe, so it was at the garage being serviced. Gross. Never mind. He hoisted his satchel onto the other shoulder.

The drive ended in a sort of tiny square where there had once been a coach house, now a place of tethered bikes, the gardener's van, and some of the masters' cars. Alongside it ran a field bordered by large old trees, once the paddock for the family horses, now a good spot for pupils to let off their animal spirits out of sight of school. Nobody was doing this today, now that it had begun to rain slightly. Kit, with no audience for once, played his daily game of hurdling over the old gate, each time knocking it over and neatly replacing it on its rusty hinges.

As he landed on the field side of it, temporarily winded, an arm came round his neck and held him in an iron clamp.

Polly had waited all day. She knew that boys always emerge from their houses sooner or later, and that morning she had got herself to the Chelmarsh home in good time to catch Kit as he left for school. With luck she could have got him then, but he left by the front door, watched by some old dragon of a servant or nursemaid, who had a tiny, half-dressed girl by the hand. Poll meditated on the possibility of running round to the back after they went into the house, and snatching the small child, but then she could have lost her other quarry.

She followed him to school, keeping well behind, out

168

of sight. She had dressed inconspicuously in a drab coat, wearing no makeup. They were all peasants in a dump like this, and the last thing she wanted was to attract attention. Her thick legs were capable of fast walking whenever the boy disappeared round a corner.

Passing through the village, she grabbed a newspaper from a stand, without paying for it, and scanned it as she walked along.

Ah, there was the headline. CHILDREN'S BONES FOUND BESIDE THAMES. And FORENSIC EXPERTS HOPE TO DETERMINE THEIR DATE. And a subheadline, COULD THESE BE THE REMAINS OF THE PRINCES IN THE TOWER? and a brief summary of the known facts about the mystery of 1483. Poll laughed. People didn't know anything these days. She threw the paper into a ditch.

The boy had turned in to the entrance of what was obviously a school, among a crowd of other boys, all in uniform. Bugger. Now she'd missed him: there hadn't been one chance during the journey to catch up with him and drag him aside.

After the stream of boys had vanished into school, Poll followed, as far as the section of the drive where the bicycles and cars were. She shrank back as a late straggler rushed in, parked his bike, and ran towards the school entrance. Then she saw the gate, and the old paddock beyond. Perfect. In a flash she was behind the gate and among the trees. They were fronted by a wall, which kept her invisible from the road. She would have a hiding place for as long as it took.

Except that it was dead boring. Nothing to do, nothing to eat—she cursed herself for bringing no fodder with her, and thought angrily of the rich store in her bedroom. (At least *he* couldn't get at it; that was some comfort.) She had passed no shops since the village. It would be possible to go back there and buy something, but that would lead to notice being taken of her.

Fate condescended to her once, when a milkman called with his daily assignment of dairy goods for the school. She watched him go up the drive swinging his metal basket, then made a lightning raid on his milk float, abstracting two bottles of milk and a carton of yogurt.

With these to sustain her, she passed the long hours until four o'clock. Then, to her relief, she saw the boys beginning to emerge. Her sharp eyes scanned each face. She had to spot him. She'd had a good look at him when he said goodbye to the woman at home. He was strikingly like his mother, and fortunately wore glasses—that made it easier. Thin, though, not like some of these beefy giant kids who could have played for Milwall.

There he was, at last, talking to another boy and walking slowly. She crept nearer and nearer the gate. To her gratification they stopped near the tethered bicycles, still talking. By now most of the others had disappeared, as briskly as boys do when the final bell has gone.

The other boy finally looked at his watch, mounted his bike, and rode off. Kit thought about his customary gate-hurdle, which to him was a sort of good-luck exercise, put down his satchel, set off on his run-up, and was over, dragging down the top bar of the gate, as usual, at which the gate obediently fell down.

Poll's strong arm held him in a viselike grip. Through his mind went the flash of a long-past conversation with his father about the iron collars worn by Saxon slaves, and how much they must hurt. He knew now how much. The arm pressed on his windpipe, arrested his breathing and swallowing, and caused spots and flashes of light to erupt before his eyes. He tried to speak, choking. The only instant explanation for this must be that he'd been grabbed by another boy, someone with a grudge against him, who had hidden and sprung. Then he heard the voice.

"So I got yer, didn't I. Didn't 'alf make me wait. Ain't you like yer mum, and won't she be sorry when they finds it. 'Cause you'll only be an It by then, like them things in the sand. Come on, don't let's make it too easy for 'em."

He felt himself painfully dragged by the neck up the sloping root of one large tree, towards the curtain wall. His heart was beating violently. He knew very certainly that his was going to be the fate of those children who spoke to strangers: killed and left dead in a copse. He knew all about it in detail, what these people did to girls and what they did to boys, and why. But this was a woman; what could she want with him? Through his pain he could feel her malevolence. She hated him. Why?

"Just about the right age, too," she was saying, in a mad kind of voice. " 'Bout the same as the bigger one, Edward, him that was King. Well, it won't be pillers and bolsters for you. Somethin' else."

Kit was an extremely cerebral boy and had read a lot of thrillers. He knew his only chance was to play dead. He could see her face close to his, ugly, like one of the terrifying Ugly-Wuglies out of E. Nesbit, and he was very frightened. But he made himself shut his eyes and go limp. At which, as he'd hoped, her grip relaxed and she leaned back, and playfully stabbed his wrist with the kitchen knife he had glimpsed in her hand. Seldom did she have the chance of contemplating a victim. (Her last, old Mal, had gone into the water without a struggle. But then his neck was broken.)

"Nah," she said, "you're goin' to feel this, not like what the dentists say. And remember, when it goes in, what they done to Black Will, how he was cheated and never got the chance to do *this*."

As she raised the knife, Kit's knee came up with a strong jerk and caught her in the stomach, winding her and sending the knife flying. Kit was on his feet in a second, slim and slight and strong as he was, and in his second year as a student of karate, of which the school had a notable teacher. He pinioned her arms behind her back, stamped agonizingly on her instep, and had her facedown on the grass before she could do more than struggle and use words he'd never heard.

With one hand he undid his leather belt and got it round her wrists, twice, roughly securing it before he tore off his school tie and secured her ankles, then returned to the wrist tether. Ah—she had a scarf round her neck that would be a good backup. He tied it tightly enough to stop her circulation.

"Blast you to hell!" she said into the earth under her face. "God rot you! Let me up!" She began to weep, howling into the tree root that was now lacerating her face.

Kit surveyed her for a moment, then ran towards the school.

Doran was cutting up animal food when Kit came in, through the back door. She ran to him and embraced him.

"Kit, darling! Oh, how I've missed you. How wonderful to see you again."

"Hi," Kit said, and kissed her warmly.

"But how late you are—it's nearly half past five. I wanted to ring the school, but Daddy said you were sure to be having a bit of extra net practice because you've got your first match next week, haven't you. But—darling,

what have you been doing to yourself? Your neck's all
. . . and why have you got a plaster on your arm?"

"Had a bit of a fall. It was nothing."

"Nothing? It looks like something to me. Where did
you have this fall?"

"By the old gate—you know, in the drive. Is that
Boris's food? Yuck."

"Yes, and Tybalt's as well, and very nasty, it is, but so
good for them. Sorry about the stink—leave the door
open."

"Er—Mum."

"Yes, there *is* something the matter, isn't there.
Come on."

His voice came out hoarsely from his bruised throat.
"I've got someone outside. I think you ought to see him."

Sudden fear chilled Doran. It *was* trouble. "Who?"

"Mr. Hite."

Mr. Hite was the math teacher, not exactly a close
friend of Kit's. She stared at Kit. "What on earth does he
want?"

"Well, he's got somebody with him. A . . . a policeman."

As Kit went out, Doran called through the door of the
corridor that led to the study. "Rodney. Come here,
please. Kitchen. Quick."

When he appeared, almost instantly, for he knew the
note of fear in her voice, she told him rapidly what had
happened. "I wanted you here. Whatever it is."

"Yes, of course. But Kit's all right, isn't he?"

Kit reappeared, behind him Mr. Hite, a neat, calm
person difficult to associate with trouble, and a pleasant-
faced young man in uniform, looking more like a
schoolboy than a police officer. Civilities were exchanged and the two men accepted tea from Vi, who had

173

mysteriously appeared on the scene unsummoned and apparently untouched by any emotion at all. Nobody was hurt, but Miss Doran was back and things might be expected to happen.

"So what's this about?" Rodney asked.

"Well," said Hite, "Christopher came running back to school about a quarter past four, when I was still there marking papers, and told me he'd been attacked by a young woman. When he described the attack I thought it was a matter for the police and telephoned Barminster, after I'd sent two handymen down to help."

"So I came straight over," said the amiable boy, who had introduced himself as DS Doug Vane. "I found the young woman where Christopher had left her, still tied up very neatly, and put the cuffs on her until I could get her into the car. Which me and my WPC had difficulty in doing—she was pretty wild."

Doran knew all too well the identity of the young woman. "Did she say anything?"

"Only . . . well, a lot of language. We thought she must be on drugs, but there was no sign. I believe they've given her a sedative. Should be all right now."

Doran didn't care whether her son's would-be murderer was all right or not. "Where is she now?"

"In the cells at Barminster. They'll get a statement from her when she's fit, and then I expect they'll take her up to the Scrubs."

"Good idea," Doran said viciously. "Pity Newgate's gone, and Tyburn too."

Rodney saw that her fists were clenched, white at the knuckles. For the first time he fully believed the horrible story of enduring medieval revenge and repeated murder. Now that it had threatened his family it was no longer a legend, embroidered by Doran's fancy: it was all too

174

true. He put an arm round his son's shoulders and drew him close.

Kit was being altogether too calm, at ten years old, after an experience that would have led to severe upset in most adults. But they noticed that he had been trembling slightly during the interview with Hite and DS Vane. Doran slipped him a very mild sedative tablet with his tea.

"The thing is to praise him, not sympathize with him," she said to Rodney, who agreed.

"We can't lay it on too thick, really. See the conqu'ring hero, that sort of stuff." With his rich pool of quotes to draw from, he let drop references to the exploits of Richard Hannay, his boyhood idol, which Kit had seen performed in two riveting films. Bulldog Drummond, they decided, was a bit over the top, but Holmes himself had had a distinguished bout of fisticuffs with the Solitary Cyclist's nasty pursuer. Doran tried hard to think of a similar incident in Thorndyke's career, but failed. Words such as *cool, intrepid*, and *dauntless* rained down on Kit like scattered elements of the obituary of a Burma Campaign veteran, and he loved it, though too modest to say so. Vi made him a special pizza for his supper; Boris's collar was enhanced by a small Union Jack left over from some celebration, which looked very well until he ate it.

Rodney immersed himself in research on the mystery of 1483. More books littered the table, including some by the school of female novelists in love with Richard III, a passionate and verbose crew.

"I don't see it," said Doran. "He doesn't look like a murderer, true, but that doesn't put him in the sex-god category. He wouldn't get a lot of film work nowadays."

"He might," Rodney said. "Moody and broody, a natural worrier. Hannibal Lecter? What do you think, Kit?"

"What you said—he looks worried."

"If he did half the things he's credited with, he'd have good reason," said Doran grimly.

"Yet he was obviously deeply pious, anxious that the souls of the dead should rest in peace. He gave lashings of money to the Church for building chapels and things. I expect he had a Mass said for the Princes, and he revered Henry the Sixth as a saint, even if he'd murdered him . . ."

"We all have our good points," said Doran. "Kit, don't you think you ought to have a nice long bath with some of my gardenia essence before you go to bed?"

Kit, who had stiffened up painfully since his fight, was only too glad to accept the suggestion, having been assured that it wouldn't make him smell girly in the morning.

Doran resisted the urge to go with him. After what had happened she dreaded his being out of her sight. Ordinarily she would have joined Rodney in his enthusiastic research, but for once she cared more for what might happen to the living than what had happened to the dead.

Out of habit she switched on the television news. Wars, as usual, in places one had never heard of.

"Curious, isn't it," Rodney said. "Things haven't changed a lot since Henry the Fourth's time. They're still breathing 'short-winded accents of new broils, To be commenc'd in strands afar remote.' "

"Shh. Listen."

A prison van and scurrying policemen filled the screen. The newsreader was saying, "A woman prisoner escaped from police custody this evening. Polly Had-

176

dock, aged about nineteen, successfully fought prison officers taking her to a remand center in South London, after a violent attack on a schoolboy in Kent. She had been put under sedation and her handcuffs temporarily removed when the bid for freedom was made. She evaded pursuit and her whereabouts are not known. The public is warned that she is dangerous and should not be approached. She is about five feet three in height, strongly built, with short brown hair and blue eyes. Wears spectacles."

They stared at each other, two masks of horror. Rodney said, "Oh Christ!" something he would never normally say out of context.

"Escaped," said Doran dully. "She *would*. Sedated or not. She's got the cunning of the Devil. I've sometimes thought she *is* the Devil."

"One of his children. What are we going to do?"

"Guard Kit. In case she comes back. She might. She could be on her way now."

"But why should she want Kit?"

"Partly because of me, I think. She doesn't like me and she thinks I interfered with her . . . domestic arrangements. And partly because she's carrying out the family oath of vengeance—killing people—children." Doran buried her face in her hands. Rodney moved to sit by her and hold her while she wept.

"I'm sorry . . . I didn't mean to cry . . . but it's all so awful! Suppose—Rodney, she could come for Armorel as well!"

He kissed and patted her, shaken by his own fear and anger, searching wildly for a solution, a net to catch the beast that ravened for their children. A small girl slept upstairs; a small boy soaked his bruised limbs, who might if the creature had her way be as dead as the bones

177

on Wapping shore, once as alive and beautiful as Armorel and her brother. When Doran was calmer he gently moved her head from his shoulder.

"Listen. We can't keep the children prisoner. It would be impossible, and they'd be frightened anyway. We've got to keep a round-the-clock watch on them somehow."

"If only we still had Sam!" mourned Doran. Sam Eastry was their onetime village constable, their community bobby and a personal friend, who had taken a fatherly interest in Doran since she first came to the district, and had been extremely useful in many of the tight corners she had got herself into. But Sam, after a breakdown, had retired into private life in a pretty cottage in the village, happy in his wife, Lydia, and his daughter, Jennifer; comparatively happy in his son, Ben, who, contrary to everyone's expectations, had followed his father into the police force.

"Ben!" exclaimed Rodney. "He's at home, I know—I saw him roaring about on that horrible machine of his last week, looking for trouble, only now it's his job to stop it instead of starting it. Just the man. He can be Kit's minder."

"His *what*? He won't like that."

"He won't be asked. One of us will drive him to school and collect him, and Ben can loom over him and look formidable. Which won't take much effort, he must be six feet three and fourteen stone. Right. I'll ring Ben now and we'll start tomorrow. I'll pay Ben, of course, can't expect summat for nowt."

Doran giggled. "I love it when you're masterful—and when you try out accents you can't do. Got any plans for Armorel—such as putting her in a convent?"

"Where do you find a convent nowadays? No, I think we can cope there."

178

They went to bed relieved in mind, feeling as though they had battled through a great storm. But the storm still raged, in the distance, keeping Doran sleepless in the dark.

For where, in all this anxious turmoil, did Will figure? And how was she to protect him?

Chapter 11

Ben Eastry appeared before time next morning, gigantic in leathers and helmet, grinning and solemn by turns. His had been a fraught boyhood, worrying to his parents, and he was delighted to be regimented at last and trusted with this nice little (paid) job for his dad's old friends.

He rode before Doran's car like an outrider on some royal progress, attracting flattering attention from schoolboys and others en route. At the entrance to the school drive he ostentatiously immobilized his bike and took an official glance at the site of the attempted crime.

"Dirty fighters, are women. Use their teeth and nails as soon as . . ." He modified his remark out of deference to his charge's youth. "As soon as look at you. You ought to've got your thumbs in her eye sockets, you know—they can't stand that."

"I know, but I didn't have time. I say, Ben," he added in an undertone, conscious of listening, fascinated ears. "I feel a bit of a fool like this. Couldn't you sort of look a bit as if you're not with me?"

"Who'm I supposed to be with, then? Your ma told me to keep close up to you as far as the school door, and that's what I'll be—close. Right, move."

On her way home, Doran bought a clutch of morning papers. She and Rodney scanned them together. With few exceptions they had picked up on the Richard III connection. One tabloid had, by some means known only to the press, got up to the enclosed area where the exhumation was being conducted, arriving fortuitously at the moment when the bones had been laid out on ground sheets in roughly anatomical order. This would give the police information about any major bones that might be missing, still buried. It also gave the photographer the most gruesome picture his paper had ever published; he hoped for a two-page spread, but they only gave him one, and it was not page three.

ARE THESE THE PRINCES IN THE TOWER? ran the caption, directing interested readers to another page, where the briefest information about the Princes was followed by the observation that even if they were not, they were somebody's children. Et cetera.

They looked, with horrified fascination, at the reassembly. The two bodies were side by side, one slightly taller than the other.

"Twelve? Nine?" Rodney measured them with his eyes. In his parish years he had seen plenty of young corpses, though none in this state. "They don't look big enough."

"People were smaller then."

"Even so. And there's no sign of the diseased jaw the elder one was supposed to have."

"That was the 1674 discovery. And it was only a stain. It probably wouldn't show up in a newspaper photograph."

"And the union of the something with something else in the skull—I can't remember anatomy parts—should one be able to see that?"

"Not without examining the actual bones, assuming that you knew what you were looking for." Doran shivered. "Edward was said to be tall for his age, handsome and charming, like his father. You'd hardly think so now. And little Richard was a mischief, a cheerful imp. Remember Olivier and the child, and those jokes about 'little'?"

"I remember Olivier and every shot in that film."

" 'Because that I am little, like an ape' . . . How hideous bones are."

"Yes." Rodney was imagining St. Crispin's churchyard, picturesque and peaceful. It didn't do to think of what lay beneath the green grass and weathered stones.

"Rodney." Doran's voice was sharp.

"Yes?"

"I don't know a lot about anatomy, but it seems to me there are an awful *lot* of bones here."

"Well, there would be."

"No, no. I mean, more than there ought to be, after the time they've been buried."

"We don't know how long."

"I'm not talking about 1483. Those are old bones, by any standards—I've seen them close up. There are two tides a day in the Thames. The burial doesn't seem to have been very far down, so how come the skeletons are so complete? Both lower jaws there, though they've got detached from the skulls—a lot of teeth—and complete sets of fingers, from what you can see here. Those are what go missing from most bodies that have been buried a long time—they get washed away or carried off by creatures, unless the whole skeleton's contained in something like a coffin. And there's no coffin here."

"How do you know?"

"I didn't see one. And it's something you'd notice,

even not in prime condition. Why don't we look at the other papers, and see what they say?"

Rodney agreed, folding the tabloid so that the picture couldn't be seen, relieved to put it out of sight. He was sickened by the horrid depiction of what might have happened to his own children, if madness and murder had had their way.

In a serious newspaper, one that gave plenty of space to archaeological finds, was a long article by a forensic expert—so long that he must have stayed up all night to write it, Rodney thought. It pointed out that a carbon test would be impossible on bones of such recent origin. ("They looked anything but recent," commented Doran, "but I suppose he knows what he's talking about.")

The age of the children would also be near impossible to determine. They were at an awkward stage when the union or ossification of certain bones might not have taken place. The dentition would, of course, be a useful and reliable guide, and the fact that so many of the teeth were present could help in this. The skeletons on the whole were remarkably intact.

This led the writer on to discuss the condition of the 1674 bones now in the Abbey. They, it seemed, had been kicked around by workmen, mixed up with chicken bones from the kitchen (or part of the workmen's elevenses? wondered Doran), and stolen.

"That urn in the Abbey ought to be opened," she said. "Modern science could analyze them at once—they may even be able to carbon-test by now."

"Tell that to the Dean and Chapter," said Rodney. "You'll get the same answer as the people got who wanted to dig up Spenser in case the Bard had tossed a tribute in at the funeral. Signed W. Shakspere or Shagsber or practically anything beginning with S. No

183

takers for that one. Yet at one time they used to let departed royals lie about while their tombs were being redesigned. That's how Pepys came to kiss Katherine of Valois."

"Pepys would kiss anything in a skirt, even if it had a shroud on top," said Doran. "Ugh! I'm getting to hate this case."

"It puts everything in a sort of bony light, like Mr. Venus's taxidermy salon," murmured Rodney, trying to stave off horror by facetiousness, as his habit was.

"Don't mention it, my unfavorite bit of Dickens. Those poor little birds . . ." Her eyes moved to the end of the newspaper article. It stated that even the sex of the bones could not be established, as they were prepubertal.

Not even the sex. So they might be . . .

A train of thought was lit in her mind. She was conscious of nothing else, not even that Rodney had slipped away to beg Armorel from Vi, so that she could play in the study while he worked. The spark burned steadily, leading on to a thought grimmer than any she had yet reached.

Where was Poll now? One would think her priority would be to go into hiding rather than to make another attempt on Kit. But where? Unless the police had done some very thorough homework, it would be difficult to trace her movements in Brighton. But perhaps they had.

DI Moray was not in, the desk sergeant told her when she spoke to the Dockland station. Any inquiries about the find at Wapping should be made direct to the Yard.

After five minutes on the Yard's busy line (or one of them), Doran felt like Shelley's cuckoo, a wandering voice. She was passed from one office to another until a

184

woman who at least sounded kind and knowledgeable agreed to talk and seemed to know the answers.

Not too helpfully. No, Haddock had not been recaptured, and there was no news of her whereabouts. Doran was thanked for the Brighton tip, which would be followed up: the voice agreed that it held possibilities. The voice was crisp, and itched to hang up on this caller.

But Doran, thinking furiously and turning on charming small talk, had made a momentous decision. It was more than likely that Poll had gone to ground at the old house. It was Doran's duty to tell the police to look for her there, so why hadn't she done so, last night? Not out of compunction for the girl, far from it. Yet she was oddly reluctant to give away that address. In the second of time between one sentence and another, all was clear to her. Will was her treasured secret. She must keep him from the eyes of the world, and especially from Rodney's. But that was wicked nonsense! He was a prisoner there, with a murderess for jailer; he must be set free. Poll would be prepared for a police raid, would fight and try to kill again, but it needn't involve Will, and from there on he must take his chance and Doran must take hers.

She said, not hesitating now, "I do know a London address where you might find Poll Haddock."

The voice was sharply interested. "Oh. Where?"

"Staple Lane, Limehouse. I think it's Number Two. You may have to break in."

"I see. Thank you. That would be S-t-a-p-l-e Lane, right? I'll tell somebody at once." Sounds of activity, voices, the woman turning away to call to someone, then back to Doran. "Your name and address, please? Telephone number? Thank you."

"You'll let me know?" Doran managed to say before

185

being cut off, and heard a crisp, "Yes, you may be needed as a witness," before the line went dead.

So she had done it: she had led them to Will. From now on she would have to lie and lie; and Will would be free. She could arrange for him to be taken away from that place, to have treatment and proper food. The weary monotony of his days would be ended. Visions of his new life flitted through her mind; she saw his rare smile, his silent delight in enjoyment. Surely he would have no feelings of pity for Poll, certainly when he knew her crimes. He had never betrayed her, but he could only be vastly relieved that her squat shadow no more loomed over him.

Perhaps some rescuing body would take over the old house, find out its history, restore it to a medieval monument but with modern amenities so that Will could still live in it. Mentally Doran installed a stair-lift, a modern bathroom, a more or less new top floor so that the bedroom could be his . . . There'd have to be extensive building works, of course, with all that dry rot and probably colonies of worm. While the works were in progress, Will could be recuperating—no, not with her, that wouldn't do, but somewhere by the sea, in a hotel on the heights above Eastgate.

She kept Rodney out of these mind pictures. He would like Will, sympathize with him, be passionately interested in the historical connections, perhaps gain himself a niche in Fame's hall by finding out more about Richard and the Princes than had been known before.

But a friendly alliance between him and Will, she couldn't see and didn't want. They were in different compartments of her life.

To distract herself she went into the garden and began to pick herbs for the evening meal. Kit, who was fortu-

186

nately not as committed to bangers and chips as most boys, liked a pie she made with vegetables from their garden, and some were available as early as this, thanks to the moisture and mildness of the spring. How delicious were young pearly potatoes from the ground, tiny onions, and the delicate little carrots that only slightly resembled their grown-up relatives. They would have quiche for lunch, sprinkled with fresh chives. And there were plenty of flowers to pick.

All this pastoral activity kept her mind clear of preoccupations, until the telephone rang. Someone would answer it. She heard Rodney come out of his study and pick it up. His voice was soft and deep, not carrying, apart from his pulpit delivery. She strained to hear, but caught only, "Yes. I see. Really." And then, "I'll call her."

His voice had not sounded happy, and his face was serious as he handed over the instrument. "For you. Scotland Yard."

The person at the other end was obviously someone with a lot of authority. Doran failed to catch his name, but it sounded like Philipson. He began with routine questions—was she sure that the attacker of her son was the same girl who had worked at 52 Copenhagen Court? Had she seen any proofs or evidence that the girl had also attacked Malcolm Grover? Had she yet been able to speak to Mrs. Evans, who had known Malcolm Grover well? Because the Yard had so far not been in contact with her.

"No. Wales is an easy place to hide in. But have you got Poll Haddock? Was she at Staple Lane?"

"No. What we need is information about her, and we need it in a hurry. I'd be much obliged if you could tell us all you know."

All? On the telephone? It would take hours and sound like a fairy story. There was an alternative, at which her heart leapt.

"I could come up to town, if you like. I could be at Charing Cross in just over the hour." She glanced at her watch. "There's a fast train from Barminster at noon."

"Well, if you're sure, Mrs. Chelmarsh. It would be much more satisfactory. A police car will meet you and take you to Staple Lane."

"Not to the Yard?"

"No. We've got a team working there, and I'm going there myself."

"Oh, good. I'll—see you then, Mr.—er."

Rodney had been standing by the hall window, not even pretending not to listen. "So you're going back to London?"

"I must. You heard—they want me to give evidence, on the spot, because I'm the only person that knows—"

"You'll leave the children again?" His voice was as grim as his face.

"Oh, Rodney. I have to! Kit won't mind; he's so sensible, and he'd want this wretch caught. Armorel won't know—tell her I've had to go out and I'll be back tonight."

"And will you?"

"I don't *know*, do I? Look, I'm very sorry, it's not my doing, but I can't refuse, I'm all mixed up in something as usual. I'll miss my train if I don't go now. Your car's working again, so you and Ben can fetch Kit. I really have to fly, tell Vi, I haven't time . . ."

Rodney watched as she hurried to her car, which was standing in the drive, got in, and drove off, without a backward look, a wave. He'd said, "You'll leave the children," but not "You'll leave me." While she had been home they had chattered as usual but had never talked about themselves, their separation. Last night they had not made love, tired and emotionally spent as they were by Kit's escape. He had missed her terribly, had got her back, and lost her again: to what? a mystery, a murder? *Had she come all the way for this. To part at last without a kiss* . . . He smiled at himself, a bitter smile. There he was, using other men's words again, poor old Topsy Morris this time, who knew all too well what it was to part without a kiss.

He went back to his study. Armorel had climbed up onto his chair and was picking letters out on his word processor. "No, no, darling." Gently he lifted her down and kissed her soft cheek. Somebody might as well get kissed . . .

Doran caught the train, after a scramble. She had snatched up an art-and-antiques magazine as she left, and turned its pages mechanically during the journey. *Suspect Caravaggio. Flood of export Chinese porcelain hits the market. Hester Bateman cream jug discovered in car boot sale.* Only a few years ago she'd have read it all with interest, even excitement. Now . . .

Station after station passed sedately, smoothly. When the train halted for no apparent reason outside a station, Doran fumed with exasperation. At the approach to London she collected her few belongings as fussily as a Victorian traveler with sixteen pieces of baggage.

Charing Cross, quiet as a village station. There in the forecourt was the squad car, stately authority beyond parking regulations. A keen-eyed officer spotted her and was at her side. How did he know her? It was his job.

"Mrs. Chelmarsh?"

"Yes."

They were in the car, speeding along with a swift

189

certainty she had never met before. Her escort sat with the driver, she in the back knowing how those people feel who are dimly seen in television newsreels with coats and blankets over their heads. Nice to be on the right side of the law.

The City, the tower blocks and their glittering window-panes, St. Katherine's Dock and Canary Wharf; and suddenly the little turning that led to Staple Lane. There the car stopped and the young officer held the door for Doran to alight.

Suddenly everything was different. The front door that had been always shut was open, the dark staircase lit; upstairs, figures were moving about and a bright electric light shone, then was moved away. A small crowd of office workers and idlers parted to let the DC and Doran through.

"Who are all these people—in the house, I mean? It looks so strange . . ."

"SOCO—scene-of-crime officers, madam. Don't worry; it's always a bit of a scrum." A tall man in plain clothes met them on the stairs, and introduced himself as the person she had thought of as Philipson, who was actually Fillotson, as if it mattered.

The old living room was a mass of movement. White-overalled figures milling about, apparently packing up things, measuring and marking things. Fillotson was saying, ". . . go somewhere quiet," which seemed an impossibility, until he preceded her into the fireplace end of the galley, where nobody seemed to be doing anything for the moment. At a slight jerk of the head from Fillotson, a very pretty WPC appeared and sat inconspicuously near them. Doran looked round eagerly for any sign of Will, but obviously they would have got him out of this melee.

"So you haven't found her—Poll Haddock," Doran said.

"No, but we found a lot of things belonging to her—or rather *not* belonging to her. That room up there is like a thieves' kitchen. And one of the owners of the stuff was the late Malcolm Grover. God, Bridget, it's mayhem in here—why did nobody tell me it was going to be like this?"

"Sorry, sir."

"I'm afraid we can't talk to you properly in this row, Mrs. Chelmarsh. We'll have to go and sit in my car, after all. Come on, Bridget."

Will's invalid chair was not in its old place, but as they left the galley she saw it in a corner. Someone had turned it upside down—how odd.

In Fillotson's large Rover it was utterly quiet except for faint street noise coming through the open window. Doran leaned back, feeling as though she had been through a food blender. She shared the backseat with Fillotson, while Bridget occupied the front, on her knee a large, boxlike thing which Doran recognized as recording apparatus. Bridget turned her beautiful dark face towards Fillotson, and her hand hovered over the switches.

"Just before we start," Doran said, "could you tell me where Mr. Slater is?"

"Mr. Slater?"

"Poll's uncle. He lived here. He was in a wheelchair. Is he all right?"

Perhaps Fillotson heard the tremble in her voice. "You don't know, then?"

"I don't know anything."

"Well. When our people broke into the house it was empty, except for a man lying at the foot of the stairs to the top landing. He was dead—had been for some hours."

Doran asked calmly. "How?"

"Broken neck. He seems to have been trying to crawl up the stairs, which were partly broken, several banisters on the ground. He was crippled—perhaps you know."

"Yes, I do."

"We think he was trying to get at food supplies in the bedroom—we found a lot of stuff up there, some of it melting from frozen, and several bottles of wine."

"The chair. The wheelchair. Where was it?"

"In the room looking onto the river—turned upside down."

After a long pause, in which the world changed and many years went by, Doran said, "I hope you catch her."

WPC Bridget O'Hara, trained to notice things such as a person's change of complexion to livid white, glanced at Fillotson and said, "I'll get in the back with you. Now—have a taste of this." She produced a neat little flask and Doran drank from it. Fillotson tactfully left the car and hovered, leaving the passenger door open. Doran wondered why there was such a loud buzzing in her ears, and why she was gripping someone's hand tightly. Bridget asked in her soft Irish voice, "Did you know him well?"

"He was . . . a friend. I found him in a . . . poor state. So I got him those things to eat. I fed him until Sunday. I thought he would be . . . all right."

Fillotson, who had been listening, said, "His niece must have come back, taken his chair away, and put the foodstuffs out of his reach."

"So he . . . crawled. But how could he?"

"God knows. His legs had been badly broken, multiple fractures, some years ago, and the bones had never been set properly. That much, our surgeon found out last night. Where was he when you left him?"

"In bed." It was only a whisper.

"It must have taken a tremendous effort to get out of the bed and as far as the kitchen—even to get the door open. Even so, he couldn't reach the tap and there was no food left downstairs. Then he—somehow—got back to the stairs. He must have known the food was up there. Hard to make neighbors hear in that place, I imagine. Office premises both sides?"

Doran nodded.

"The door to the downstairs entrance was locked, and so was the front door. She was planning to stay away a long time."

Bridget unobtrusively crossed herself before she took Doran's shaking body in her arms. Fillotson said, "Take Mrs. Chelmarsh back to the squad car, Constable, and drive her wherever she wants to go. Stay with her."

Doran steadied herself. "I want to go back into the house. Please, will you take me?"

The SOCO team had nearly finished their work, though one or two white-coated women remained, making lists, it seemed. Doran walked slowly through to the galley, looked out of the window, where he used to sit. Careful not to touch anything, she made herself go to the foot of the broken staircase. There on the wooden floor was the outline of a recumbent figure, so familiar from films and book jackets, drawn in adhesive tape. One arm was out-thrown and the head was turned, lying in profile. It seemed to have no connection with Will.

Bridget said, "We did find something else when we opened up, Mrs. Chelmarsh. A bird."

"Oh no! Not Grip?"

193

"Don't worry, he was alive—just. We think he'd found some—insects and things."

"Thank God. Where is he?"

"They've taken him to a vet to look after."

"Will you ask them to keep him, for me? He's a Tower raven and he was a . . . pet. Where was he?"

"In the basement room. Pretty grisly down there, isn't it."

"I thought it was like a tomb."

Fillotson said, "Possibly it was, once. We found traces—but I don't think we ought to discuss that now. Will you get Mrs. Chelmarsh home, Bridget. All the way, if necessary."

By eight o'clock that evening Doran was sitting by her own parlor fire. She had absolutely refused to go to bed, even after being brought home in a police car, having been in no state to be questioned, the original intention of her visit to London. Rodney was shocked by the effect the experience had had on her. Poor Kit, struggling with his homework, wondered when things were ever going to be normal again and when he could go to and from school unescorted by Ben, who was beginning to enjoy his position as minder rather too enthusiastically.

And Doran, a living proof of the triumph of the human spirit, was telling Rodney all she knew about the black saga of the Slaughter family.

Chapter 12

Rodney and Vi (who surely deserved a full explanation after the disturbances of the past week) listened to what was possibly the most unsavory story either of them had heard. Vi read plenty of horrors in the daily and Sunday tabloids, but they had no emotional reality for her. Things that happened to unknown people only produced a shiver at one remove. This was something terrible that had happened to her Miss Doran, to whom she maintained an almost feudal loyalty.

For her benefit Doran merely outlined the episode of Black Will and the missed reward. Vi knew as much about Richard III and the Princes as everybody did, or thought they did. She found the inherited oath difficult to take in. "But they must have been mad," she declared, "stark staring mad."

"Oh, I think they were, at first. Then it became a family tradition. I shouldn't wonder if it went by the board a few times, as people got more scrupulous or more scared—it wouldn't be too easy to say why you'd killed two children you'd happened to meet in a deserted spot."

"Children!"

"I think it was mostly children. They were very expendable in those days, you know—unwanted ones could go into the river or onto a rubbish heap without too much being said." Doran was thinking of the whores of Bankside and the by-blows they must have produced, whatever their skill in the preventive arts. Vi looked extremely shocked. She had once lost a niece by psychological murder.

Rodney said, "But Mal Grover was hardly a child."

"No, he was part of the robbery element, carving up wealthy merchants and taking their gold and jewels to compensate for the lost reward." She told them about the police discovery of treasures in Poll's room. "She probably kept them up there until she could find the right fence. It isn't easy, even in Brighton. When I was a dealer I got to know the feel of hot property, or more likely of the people who brought it in—though I got done several times."

"So what happened to all these riches?" asked Rodney.

"You tell me. They didn't go on high living, certainly. My bet would be on a hoard somewhere."

"That filthy old house!" Vi snorted. "Just the place to hide things, I'd guess. Secret hiding places—priests' holes."

"They'd hardly need those. I expect when the country went Protestant the family sent one person to church every Sunday, to avoid awkward questions from the Bawdy Court."

Vi was even more shocked. Doran reassured her. "Oh, that was only the official inquiry into how often you went to church and to Communion, that sort of thing. It was also useful for catching secret Catholics. And as for the hoarded riches, if they're anywhere, the police will find them—they'll turn that place inside out."

Rodney was seriously concerned. This was how Doran would behave under inquisition, with the rack waiting in the corner and the gallows outside. He tried a test question. "And what was Will's role in all this?"

"I think he was a refuser of the oath. His father's first wife died and the children were 'lost.' He married again, his wife ran away, and the son refused. I think the father waited till he was a grown man and then told him he'd have to make up his mind—not for the first time, I imagine—in fact, I'm sure."

"And—?"

"And he refused again, firmly, and his father lost his temper and—did something to him." Her eyes met Rodney's, defying him to see any involved emotion in them. "My theory is that he threw him downstairs, possibly down the ones that go down to the front door, which finish on a stone floor. His legs were broken in several places, including one hip. Then he was left, not given medical attention or surgery."

"But you don't *know* this."

"I know from what I know of the people concerned. Then the girl, Poll, was appointed Keeper of the Oath or whatever they called it, and trained by her grandfather. She was a bit young, but it doesn't seem to have stood in her way."

"And she was what relation?"

"Niece. Daughter of Will's sister, the one who ran away."

"I don't know how such things could happen in this day and age!" burst out Vi.

"They didn't happen in this day and age," Rodney said. "They happened in what used to be called the Dark Ages, though now we call them Middle Ages. Middle of what, I wonder? Civilization? It's astonishing, though, that the oath could be kept alive all those centuries—

when you think of little things like the law, and changes in morality. Well, I can only say I hope you're wrong."

"I hope so too. But I don't think I am. And it won't alter what's happened." Nothing will alter that . . .

"Why don't we all have a hot nightcap, down here?" Rodney suggested brightly. "We could use the best silver and bring out the Glenfiddich, and pretend we were in India."

Vi looked doubtful. "Well, I don't know. I think I'll stick to my malted milk."

"If we were in India, we wouldn't be having a hot nightcap," Doran said. "Let's be Errol Flynn and his mates in a villa on the Costa Cirrhosis, and have old-fashioneds. You make a really deadly one, Rodney, and there's some pineapple juice in the fridge and one bottle of rye left. Come on."

Rodney prepared the drinks, which were truly lethal, and Doran's sleep was a blessed oblivion.

DI Fillotson, a chivalrous man, suggested that Doran might prefer to make her deferred statement at her local police station rather than travel up to town again. She willingly agreed. At the graceful Georgian building that was Barminster's nick she was accommodated with a small, quiet room, a WPC sitter-in (like doing exams in the presence of an invigilator, she thought), and a type-writer to save her the labor of scribbling pages by hand.

She put down all the facts, from her first encounter with Poll to her last visit to Staple Lane, leaving out all reference to her relations with Will. Finally she added a section laying out her own theories; they could take those or leave them, as they wished.

DI Fillotson read it with approval next day. Not often he got anything so balanced and articulate, even if parts of it sounded over the top. But in this case perhaps very little rated as over the top. There had been developments overnight that he very much wanted to pass on to this invaluable witness. It happened that the articulate Mrs. Chelmarsh was very much his type of woman. Her breakdown at Staple Lane had touched a heart that years of life in the force had not managed to transform into massive rock, unmov'd by sentimental shock, as the feigned Leonard Meryll of *Yeomen* declared his to be; and she had very beautiful legs. One should always notice a witness's feet, said the guide to the successful interviewing of witnesses and suspects, and there seemed no reason why legs should be excluded from the survey.

Which was why he telephoned her personally at home, even offering her paid accommodation in a small hotel off Victoria Street, which she refused.

She asked Rodney, "Shall I go? Will you mind?"

"No, I don't mind. Which isn't to say I wouldn't rather you stayed here, but their wish is a command, isn't it." *And,* he added silently, *you have something to work out on your own account, Doran.*

The only person who objected strenuously was Kit. Normally obedient and ready to see reason, he demanded to go up to town with his mother.

"I'm a witness too, and I was the attacked person. I think I ought to have a bit of the action. Somebody ought to interview me. It's Friday and there's nothing special doing at school. Besides, I want to see Scotland Yard."

Doran sighed. "Scotland Yard isn't what you think. It's really rather dull, and you'd hate all the waiting about. If I have to talk, you'll make me nervous, just by being there. I'll take you in the Easter holidays, if you like, but not tomorrow, *please*."

Kit knew when he was beaten. Still slightly mutinous,

199

he went off to school, his objections partly mollified by having been promoted to being a passenger on the back of Ben's bike.

As it happened, there was almost no waiting. Fillotson had arranged the interview for a reasonably elastic time in the morning, with no meetings impending or important calls expected. He thought Doran looked much better than last time he had seen her, devastated by shock. Her manner, disappointingly, was friendly but formal, raising no hopes of the lunch that had hovered pleasantly in his thoughts.

He seated her comfortably on a small two-seater couch which had the double advantage of making VIP visitors aware that they were not sitting in an interview room, like common criminals, and of being in a good light, which did a lot for her hazel curls, her nymph's figure in a dress the color of a black pearl, and the really distinguished legs. He wondered why a woman like that would marry a vicar. But of course, she was given to good works, wasn't she.

After congratulating her on her statement, he said, "I realize, and I'm sure you must, that quite a bit of it was supplied by your imagination."

"I'm sorry. I'm afraid it got out of hand."

"Not as much as you may have thought. I have news for you, Mrs. Chelmarsh. Poll Haddock has been arrested."

"What!"

"Yes. True. She wasn't very clever, you know. Cunning but not clever, and our Brighton police have had a lot of experience in sniffing out her type. Your Brighton tip was invaluable. She must have gone straight down there after her escape."

"And she didn't know I'd been told it was her hideout."

"No."

"Her . . . uncle told me."

"I see. Well, we'd held her once, so we knew exactly what she looked like—no question of mistaken identity."

"And she wouldn't be a mistress of disguise, would she—too many limitations."

"Right. She looked the way she did, and she had a good few bruises we traced back to your son."

"Oh, good, he'll be pleased."

"Quite a boy, that. We'd had this word about a house in Brighton, back-street place, not the posh waterfront kind, where stuff on the hot list usually finishes up and gets sold off if the thief can't find a reliable fence. Well, Poll, it seems, had a room there—not rented but on a sort of friendly arrangement."

Doran could guess the arrangement: a room where Poll could take clients when she had time on her hands, paid for on a percentage basis.

"It seems our boys just walked in, casually, and nabbed her. I won't say she came quietly, because she didn't. But we found a lot of stuff on her that was traceable back to places where she'd worked, plus a signet ring and a Rolex of Mr. Grover's—and the emerald earrings."

"She still had those, then?"

"Yes, they must have been hard to flog. For one thing, they were real emeralds, pretty valuable. For another, they were very long and an awkward shape; they'd have needed cutting up. We'll want Mrs. Evans's confirmation about them, *when* we can get hold of her, but there's not much doubt. Poll turned very nasty on our chaps and particularly on the WPC."

She would.

"But they got her, and a couple of local types—one of them well known to us—and this time there was no wriggling out of it." He breathed heavily, a reflection of his own experience of Poll Haddock in captivity. "And the most important part was, we got a statement out of her. I thought you'd like to see it."

Doran would, indeed.

"This isn't the original, in fact—we had to make a transcription. Her writing's not the best and we had to get an expert onto some of the phraseology. But this is the final result." He passed it over just as his telephone rang, leaving Doran free to read the document.

It was indeed extraordinary. It could have been read as a mad person's confession in other circumstances, but too much of it related to the story Doran had compiled from the clues. The style was as crazed as the matter. Here was the date, 1483 (she had had that impressed on her, evidently). Some of the names were misspelt and had been left as she had put them down in her crabbed scrawl. Black Will Slauter, our foregoer (forebear?). Grene, Dytone, Forest. Black Will had been "charged to care for the King and the Duke," meaning the two little boys, but his place had been taken from him and his gold denied.

So far it sounded like the original story told over and over until the child remembered the exact words, as a child would the words of a story read repeatedly at bedtime. There was more of the original matter, obviously learned by heart or from a continually refreshed copy. "When Black Will would not give up his place easily, the King's (Richard's) men bete and cudgelled him sorely and at last flung him into the river where they thought to leve him for dead. But some of his men watching nearby

202

took him out and carried him to the home of his son in Limehouse, where his back was proven to be broke but not to danger of his life.

"So he had cheated them that would murder him, and heard from the Tower that others had been given his charge, to kill the two royal infants, and this they did and got much preferment from it. Then our foregoer vowed that his son should kill two children as the others had been killed and take what spoils he could from any at Court or about the Citie in repayment for the gold he had been robbed of.

"And his son's son and all that came after him in each generation were to do the same for Black Will's sake."

So much for the Oath. The style suddenly changed to Poll's own, addressed to the police.

"Then it was up to our lot. They didn't know round Limehouse who Black Will was, only the house got a name for being cursed and people kep away right up to this year, though guys came callin to ask questions but we was too clever and put them off. That Tower warder must've heard something, he kept callin. All this went on for hundreds of years and it's in the Black Book and I'm sick of writing this stuff, look for yourselves. I will put this down, though, my granddad Dick Slater got married twice, the first wife died and left two daughters. He could see they wasn't no good, wouldn't understand the Promise or have the guts to do what it said, so he had them killed by a nephew of his. Well, that was part of the Promise he could do wasn't it. I think they was a bit soft anyway."

"The lost children," said Doran. "Oh God."

"Then," went on the statement, "he married again a lot later, but the wife couldn't stand him and ran off, leaving him with my mum and her brother, my uncle Will. They

called him Bill so that the name wouldn't remind
anybody."

"After five hundred years! Hardly likely."

"Then my mum married my dad, Jim Haddock, and
had me, but they moved away when I was little. I think
it was America they went to, anyway Granddad never
heard any more. He was real mad. My uncle didn't
want to know about the Promise, said he wouldn't do
it, so Granddad who had a bit of a temper chucked him
down the front stairs and into the street, same like
Black Will, and when they picked him up his legs was
all smashed, but Granddad said he wasn't going to get
mixed up with hospitals and all that. Anyway, he'd got
a Keeper of the Promise now, me. He said I'd got the
guts for it and I was like what they used to be in Black
Will's days."

"How right he was."

"You know what happened last week about that filthy
rich old man I got rid of. I couldn't get no children, so I
went down to our cellar and got the bits of the two girls
Granddad had seen off, all them years back—they was in
a sack under the coal—and I put them under the shingle
or whatever at Wapping and left a notice so people would
see it and know the Promise was still being kept. But you
clever lot thought it were little King Edward and the
Duke, didn't you.

"That was really funny. I did laugh."

Doran handed back the typescript, feeling dazed and
sick.

"Her own aunts! I did wonder, once. It's true, isn't it,
that the sex of prepubertal children can't be told from
bones?"

"Quite true. And forensic found very poor cranial

development, suggesting that the sisters may have been mentally retarded or underdeveloped in some way."

Doran gulped. "I—I got some fuel from the top of that heap in the cellar, when the fire wanted mending. To think . . ."

"Yes. Forensic found traces of human . . . of bodies having decomposed not far from there. And there was a sack at Wapping, thrown away, that had obviously contained something of the kind. Mrs. Chelmarsh, you look awful. I shouldn't have shown you all this. I just thought, as an antiquarian, you'd be interested."

"Oh, I am, I am. Please don't offer me brandy, will you. People are always doing that and it makes me feel so Victorian. I don't think I want to see any more, unless you've got this Black Book handy?"

"Of course." It was one of the ancient volumes she had seen: very slim, because very few of those who had written in it were able, in the fullest sense, to write, and many of their scrawls were incomprehensible, mere names and comments and a few dates.

1535. 10 pence 1 St James broach. II watermans sons.

1599. Wm the Keeper hanged.

1620. Scotch King hunts Witches. Keeper taken but freed.

Doran returned the book to his desk. "Thank you. There's only one thing I'd like to do, which may sound silly. Have you—is Will Slater still . . ."

Fillotson was quick to understand, if not quite accurately. He had got her down as a lay Sister of Mercy, one who had helped someone in distress and wanted to pay a last tribute. Very worthy.

205

"Yes, he's at an undertaker's we sometimes use, when the victim's family don't make a claim. Burial takes place—let me see, Saturday? Yes."

"Could I see him? I'll find my own way."

"No, of course not, one of our girls will take you."

He did some telephoning. The girl, when she appeared, was Bridget O'Hara. Doran was delighted to see her, and Bridget's smile was warm as sunshine on practically any dark range of Irish mountains you cared to name, thought Doran.

Leaving Fillotson's office, she turned and said, "You'll get her, won't you—Poll? She won't slip off the hook on a plea of unsound mind?"

"No, she won't. She'll get the maximum, unless I'm much mistaken. You'll be called as a witness in any case."

"Thank you. I shall enjoy that."

With Bridget still at her side, she went into a small, very quiet room lit by electric candles. The undertaker's receptionist was a cozy woman of infinite tact and discretion. She was not sure of the status of this visitor, but said exactly the right things. Bridget melted out of the room with her.

He was in what Doran supposed was a coffin, but gave a curious impression of being a sailor's bunk, neatly covered with a purple pall. An open shirt gave him a slightly Shelleyesque look. His face was quite beautiful, the faint secret smile of the dead touching his lips, the white hair sweeping back from an unlined brow. How could she ever have thought his features rough-hewn? They were marble, as from the hand of Bernini. He could have been a Plantagenet King, lying so: what irony.

She made the sign of the cross on the icy brow, and left him. To the receptionist she said, "He was a devout Catholic. Could you arrange for a priest, do you think?"

"Yes, indeed. We'd wondered, seeing the crucifix. I'm glad you told me."

Bridget whispered as they left, "The little sisters are here, too. We've got their names and dates and everything. They have a white coffin because they were so young."

"I'm glad." She had taken one of the undertaker's cards so that she could send masses of flowers: Will should not go ungarlanded. She asked the receptionist, "Where will they be buried?"

"I know that," said Bridget. "It's usually potter's field, which means paupers' graves, for victims with no families, but they're going to somewhere special. It's a bombed church that's been cleared and made into a sort of garden. There's been a lot of interest in this case, historical people calling in about it."

"So I should think. Please, will you thank . . . whoever, if you find out."

"I will that."

Sitting in the train, watching the outposts of London give way to the fields of Kent, Doran saw only what she had just seen in the candlelit room. There was a song going through her head, a sea ballad she could only remember in part, but it was coming back to her line by line.

> Now a long goodbye to Limehouse Reach,
>   And a last goodbye to you:
> A man's a fool to die for love,
>   Which I don't mean to do.

For the—something, anchor's off the ground,
　　And it's time for us to go—
But I would have loved you so, my dear,
　　I would have loved you so.

Chapter 13

As Doran put her key in the lock it was apparent that Bell House had visitors. A muffled but increasing roar, as of a cocktail party getting under way, came from the drawing room, and two of the voices in it were Welsh. Doran arranged her face with difficulty into a welcoming beam and went in.

Cries of delight greeted her from Gwenllian, who in dusky red embroidered with pearls managed to look like the enchantress Morgan le Fay, even at teatime on a dark afternoon, with Armorel sprawled across her lap wearing all her costume jewelry, chanting spontaneous tunes. They would have fitted perfectly into one of those fantasy films full of Hollywood elves and dwarves rushing about in Styrofoam caverns.

Howell welcomed Doran with a tobacco-flavored embrace. He was wearing jeans, a Scandinavian-type sweater of impenetrable thickness, and dirty trainers. There was a drink in his hand that was neither tea nor alcohol-free lager. He seemed to have the remains of a bad cold.

Doran went straight to Rodney, whose pleasure in her early return was mixed with relief that she had returned at all, after recent events. He let her out of his arms reluctantly to go to her guests. The room was littered with cups, glasses, an excited Boris and a disgusted Tybalt (on the top of a tall secretaire), a packet of Armorel's nappies, and Kit, who had rushed downstairs on hearing his mother's return. It was cheerful and noisy and just what Doran wanted.

Gwenllian was saying "... and when I heard you'd gone up on police business I said to myself, dear oh dear, will there never be an end to all this to-do I started, getting you up to that Devil's town of a place at all, but you see I had this feeling, this very strong feeling—"

"OK, Mam," said Howell, "save it. I won't say you're looking well, Doran, because you aren't, but it's good to see you."

"Oh, I'll be all right after about a month in a convalescent home. Where did you get that awful cold? Don't give it to the children, will you—Kit, there's a new box of tissues by Daddy's bed, will you get it for Uncle Howell, please, there's a lamb. So you're not a monk anymore, Howell. Or are you just having a day off in mufti?"

Howell looked shifty. "Well, it was a bit sudden, see. I got a f—fearful chill hanging about in the rain looking for Mam here, and I felt I was being a bit of a pain at the Abbey. Poor old Brother Bob's past night-nursing at his age, so I had it out with Owain, and he agreed with me that we'd be best off as business partners. I can't say I was sorry; it was none too comfortable and the hours wasn't what I was used to. I just didn't seem to fit in."

"You mean you couldn't put your feet up and read Christie's Quarterly and mend clocks all the time; you had to go and sing hymns at four o'clock in the morning?"

Howell shuddered. "Something like that. Owain was

very understanding—we parted friends. I'm not sorry—it was something I had to do."

"We all know the feeling, Howell," Rodney said. "It does you credit. Kit, what is it? Mummy's talking."

"I only wanted to know what the police said. Do they want to see me? There'll be a trial, won't there? Shall I have to be a witness?"

"Trial?" Gwenllian looked from one to the other of them.

"I really couldn't say, darling, but I don't suppose so. Rodney, would you be an angel and take the children to Vi? It's time for Armorel's bath, and I think, Kit, you should do your homework now, and then you can have an early supper with us." Rodney knew this meant "I want to give the Evanses an edited version and I don't want the children to hear it." He picked up his daughter, now totally festooned with rings, beads, and brooches. "Come on, Zenobia, you can go out like starlight, hid with jewels, and before you have your bath you can take every one of them off and give them back to Auntie Gwenllian."

Armorel began to wail. "Don't want to! Want dem!"

"Well, you can only have dem till bathtime. Out."

The room was blissfully quiet again. Tybalt descended and curled up on a bookshelf, purposely near a valuable Meissen figure. He knew this alarmed people, and he was a past master of blackmail.

"Trial?" Gwenllian repeated. "Is this something about my earrings? Is that why you had to go to Scotland Yard?"

"Your earrings have in fact been found, Gwenllian, but that's not why—"

"Who took them? Where were they found? Does Mal know?"

"Probably, taking the long view. But prepare for a shock. Gwenllian—I'm afraid Mal's dead."

"Dead! No! Was it his heart?"

"No, he was murdered—neck broken and pushed in the river." Howell laid his hand on his mother's, but she shook it off. "When?" she demanded. "Was it the night we went out?"

"Yes, and that's why he didn't come back. It was nothing to do with you." Doran took a deep breath. She was determined not to relate the whole dreadful story again, if only for her own sake. This was going to be the merest outline, to satisfy Gwenllian and Howell. "I'm sorry to say that his death was caused by Poll Haddock, and it was she who took the earrings. She turned out to be a very bad girl indeed, Gwenllian; you were right to dislike her instinctively. She was a member of a criminal family—" difficult to put, this "with a tradition of robbery and murder that went back a very long way. I got mixed up in it through looking after someone she'd—ill treated, and it all got very complicated and alarming—she even attacked Kit."

Howell choked on his drink as Doran hurried on.

"But that was all right in the end, and please tell him how brave he was because he's still dining out on it. Anyway, the police got Poll and found a lot of the stuff she'd stolen, and she's in custody awaiting trial, as they say."

"I hope she gets life that *means* life," Gwenllian said vindictively. "And that's too good for her."

"What will they get her on?" Howell asked.

"I don't know what the charge will be. Unlawful act causing death—" that was terribly true in one case "—robbery, assault with intent to kill . . . It could be anything."

"How d'you know all this?" Howell asked. "Criminal law?"

"I checked."

Gwenllian had been silent, gazing at nothing. Now she said, "Those bones, the two children they found by the river. Was that anything to do with—her?"

"In a way, yes. Very much so. Closely related." How true.

"You know, *cariad,*" said Gwenllian slowly, "all this trouble you've had is my fault in a way. I sensed you were unhappy, and why. We won't talk about it."

"No, don't let's."

"I knew you and Rodney both needed a change, and when I met Tiggy again it seemed to me she might provide the answer, if you had a break in London and Tiggy accidentally on purpose came into Rodney's life anyway. That didn't work, except that he realized he'd outgrown her and you were his mate, all he wanted. Has he told you that?"

"Yes." He had told her in his deeply considered way that he had found Tiggy changed from a charming kitten to a charming but neurotic and restless cat, a victim of her own beauty and of men. It was not her fault; she had been sent by Gwenllian on this mission to restore Rodney's youth, which she had thought from the first was not a good idea. But they had become fast friends and she had made him realize fully how badly he had neglected Doran. And then Tiggy had gone, leaving Rodney a changed man, in love with his wife again and longing for her.

Gwenllian nodded. "I think it worked, funnily enough, but I should never have done it. I was an interfering old fool." She gave Howell the "Get lost" sign he recognized instantly, and he drifted out of the room.

Gwenllian looked into Doran's eyes. "And you. I led you into great trouble. Grief."

"In the end. But into great joy too."

"Yes, I can see that. I can see it all. The pall, and the candles. Your heart."

"Thank God I don't have to tell you. Or anybody, ever. I'm not sorry; I'm glad. For both of us."

"Remember *The Yeomen*? *'His pains were o'er and he sighed no more, For he lived in the love of a lady.' "*

"You're a wise woman, Gwenllian. That's exactly how it was."

*Antiques dealer Doran Fairweather, resident of the cozy
English village of Abbotsbourne, never expected to
unearth so many murders....*

The Doran Fairweather
Mysteries

by Mollie Hardwick
Author of *Upstairs, Downstairs*

"Gracefully written and full of interesting arcana
about the antiques trade, both consistent virtues
of this unusually pleasing series."
— *The New York Times Book Review*

Published by Fawcett Books.
Available at your local bookstore.

The Doran Fairweather Mysteries

MALICE DOMESTIC
Doran Fairweather's comfortable life in the village of Abbotsbourne suits her to a T. Then a sinister stranger arrives, casting over the village a pall of evil that few can resist.

PARSON'S PLEASURE
The exquisite 300-year-old clock acquired by her partner is a find that antiques dealers would kill for—and Doran is sure that it is stolen property. Returning the clock leads her to the Cotswolds, and down a trail of violence.

UNEASEFUL DEATH
Doran Fairweather is looking forward to the two-day Antiques Roadshow at luxurious Caxton Manor. And then the snow starts to fall—complete with blocked roads, out-of-order phones, isolation, and murder.

THE BANDERSNATCH

Doran simply must have the antique rosy-lipped angel for her baby's nursery. But right after the purchase, her family's peaceful life is interrupted by irate antiques collectors and intruders—and Doran must act before it's too late.

PERISH IN JULY

Doran and her husband enjoy working on the parish's summer production of a Gilbert and Sullivan operetta—until the cast's most hated member turns up dead.

THE DREAMING DAMOZEL

Doran is elated to find an oil painting of the Pre-Raphaelite beauty Lizzie Siddal. But when she discovers a girl's body floating in a pond, she is shocked at how the scene mirrors the image of Lizzie as the dying Ophelia.

THE
DORAN FAIRWEATHER MYSTERIES
by Mollie Hardwick

Published by Fawcett Books.
Available at your local bookstore.

MOLLIE HARDWICK

Published by Fawcett Books.
Available in bookstores everywhere.

Mollie Hardwick has written six other novels in the Doran Fairweather series: *Malice Domestic, Parson's Pleasure, Uneaseful Death, The Bandersnatch, Perish in July,* and *The Dreaming Damozel.* She is also well known as the author of historical novels, especially *Upstairs, Downstairs,* which was made into a very popular BBC television series.

She lives in London, England.

Printed in the United States
by Baker & Taylor Publisher Services